R

HORSE-KETCHUM
of Death Valley

**Center Point
Large Print**

HORSE-KETCHUM
of Death Valley

DANE COOLIDGE

CENTER POINT PUBLISHING
THORNDIKE, MAINE

This Center Point Large Print edition
is published in the year 2009 by arrangement with
Golden West Literary Agency.

The text of this Large Print edition is unabridged.
In other aspects, this book may vary
from the original edition.
Printed in the United States of America.
Set in 16-point Times New Roman type.

ISBN: 978-1-60285-612-7

Library of Congress Cataloging-in-Publication Data

Coolidge, Dane, 1873-1940.
  Horse-Ketchum of Death Valley / Dane Coolidge. -- Large print ed.
    p. cm.
  ISBN 978-1-60285-612-7 (library binding : alk. paper)
  1. Death Valley (Calif. and Nev.)--Fiction. 2. Large type books. I. Title.

PS3505.O5697H67 2009
813'.52--dc22

2009024422

CONTENTS

CHAPTER I

DEATH VALLEY

DOWN a long, rocky wash, where round boulders as smooth as death-heads lay shimmering in the heat, a train of covered wagons wound its way into the West, pounding a road out with grinding wheels. Behind, by the bitter waters of the Amargosa and up through a battle-strewn pass, lay the ruins of smoking wagons, unburied dead and the litter of a losing fight. And on their flanks a horde of Indians followed along like evil spirits, patiently waiting for the end—and their loot.

The gaunt oxen, straining and groaning at the weight of their yokes, moved slowly, barely lifting their feet, though the bull-whips popped like pistol-shots. They balked, rolling their eyes at the brazen sky and the pitiless desert peaks. Then at a whiff of wind from the far abyss below they lowed and surged crazily on. There was water in the sink which opened up before them—water that seethed and gave off steam like a cauldron in the heat, water that gleamed like burnished silver in the sun. But to drink was to sup with Death.

In the lead, as crazed with heat as the oxen they belabored, rushed young men in their prime and old men full of years, helter-skelter in their race for a drink. Twenty wagons, bumping and rumbling

7

and grinding against the rocks, poured out from the canyon's mouth and dashed down the long slope that ended on the edge of the marsh. But behind and moving slowly—with the train but not a part of it—there followed a wagon equipped with barrels for water and guarded by one man, with a rifle.

He was tall and eagle-eyed, with a long, black beard; and he was mounted on a horse such as never had been seen in the West. It was a stallion, as yellow as gold, with a flowing mane and tail and a small head on a high-crested neck. And, led behind the wagon, were three more of that royal strain which comes from the deserts of Araby. Each was yellow as gold, each had slim, springy legs and the long, graceful lines of speed. And each held its head as if conscious still of the regal blood in his veins. Begotten of the desert they had returned at last to a land even sterner than their own.

Between mountains so boldly sheer that they rose like sun-blacked walls there lay a valley below the level of the sea. In its sink the bitter waters of a hundred desert draws lay steaming in a putrid marsh. Broad quicksands, white and quivering, merged at last with salt-caked flats, flanked by sand-hills where the wind leapt and played.

Then the mountains began, where from narrow-mouthed canyons great boulders as big as houses had been spouted out like pebbles before the resistless drive of cloudbursts. But on the floor of the storm-swept washes brittle shrubs had reared their heads and Selim champed at their tops as he passed. Strange memories had come back to him, latent instincts that could not die. He snuffed the desert wind and sighed.

Across the flats at a lumbering gallop the twenty wagons raced, leaving Randolph Morgan behind; but when they reached the marsh where the stinking waters gleamed they mired in the treacherous sands. There was no place for miles where man or beast could drink and the hovering Indians yelled exultantly. Yet with desperate haste the leaders dug out their teams and followed along the shore to the north.

The ground became firm, low hills rose before them where the mountains pressed in on the marshes. And between meadows of salt-grass a winding creek could be seen, where the water drained in from the west. It was like a mirage, with green trees that danced and beckoned on the margin of a winding stream, but as the oxen snuffed the breeze they surged into their yokes and ran bellowing up the valley.

Yet for all their frenzied haste one wagon was ahead of them as they ascended the last, long slope. Randolph Morgan, the stranger who had followed in their rear, had cut across the flats while they stuck. Leaving his wife to drive the oxen he went galloping up the hill to look out the valley below, and the Indians scattered before him like quail. Yet though they scattered they did not flee, and from the summit of a black butte they gazed down at him—watchful and expectant.

On the edge of the crystal stream which meandered through the meadow Morgan knelt to slake his thirst. His lips were parched and cracking, his tongue swollen, his throat dry; but as he bowed down to drink Selim sniffed at the water and threw up his head with a snort. Morgan tasted—the water was salt. Yet, salt as it was, it was sweet to heat-parched lips and he threw himself down to drink. But once more, head by head, Selim snuffed at the sparkling stream and his flaring nostrils snorted the alarm. With eyes that seemed to speak he met his master's gaze and Morgan spat the poisoned water back.

It was too clear, too clean, too devoid of vegetation and the scum of green, microscopic plants. There was a rank, fishy odor and a taste like epsom salts, and the banks were a dull, leprous white. Morgan rose up with a curse and gazed across at the swarming Indians, who were dancing on the butte-top like crows. Even now they counted him dead.

Over the brow of the hill a covered wagon came lumbering and dipped down into the valley below, while the drivers set up a cheer. But as the ox-teams rushed forward Randolph Morgan rode to meet them, waving his arms to turn them away.

"Don't drink!" he yelled. "The water is poison!

Don't drink! It will be your death!" But the drivers did not give him a glance.

For two days and two nights they had been without water, except the little in their casks and canteens. Their tongues were dry with thirst, their throats were choking, their bodies were too parched to sweat. Gaunt and emaciated, their eyes blinded by heat and dust, they drove madly down the hill and out across the flat towards the creek that flowed by, crystal clear.

Men and oxen alike plunged into the little stream and drank deep, though the water was salt. They wallowed in the mud in an ecstasy of relief, while their dried-up skins soaked in moisture. And the man who rode among them, with warning shouts that the water was bad, was thought to be crazed by the heat. Teams of oxen, dragging their chains, came running from the wagons where their drivers had turned them loose and dammed the shallow stream with their bodies.

The covered wagons gave up women, with children at their skirts; and as they knelt by the trampled shore the strange man snatched them back, while he begged them not to drink. But they laughed and drank their fill, though the water was salt, and at last he gave up in despair. Over the hill, struggling stubbornly against gad and brakes, his own oxen came in sight and he galloped to turn them back.

It was a battle from the start. The smell of water

was in their nostrils, and they saw nothing of the death-scene below. Already yokes of oxen, turned out to graze on the salt-grass, had fallen like logs on the flats. The men who drove them were sickening now, stretched out in the shade of the wagons; yet still the one team which had been saved from their fate struggled and pawed and surged at their chains. Morgan fought them till he was weary, then threw the bull-chain loose and let them go their way.

"Let them drink!" he called to his wife. "Let them die with the rest. We'll never escape alive if we wait on these cursed oxen. We must mount our horses, and ride!"

He threw a saddle on Neysa, his wife's gentle mare, and loaded the two fillies with food. And then, from the shaded wagon, he lifted out a baby and placed it in its mother's arms. On the flats below men were running in crazy circles or digging holes in the sand. They were sick, deathly sick, yet to quench their fevered thirst they crawled back to the creek to drink. And the Indians, like flapping crows, swarmed the top of the grim, black butte, impatiently awaiting the end.

A fierce wind, furnace-hot, swept down from the north, seizing the sand of the giant dunes and hurling it on high like a pillar of smoke and flame. Then the sandstorm overwhelmed them, drawing a veil over their agonies as they ran in wider circles and fell. The Indians crept closer, eager to begin the work of loot, and with an anger akin to madness Morgan charged down upon them, both pistols smoking at once. They fled to their black-domed butte, waving their arms exultantly. All was theirs—the desert had killed for them.

CHAPTER II

THE GHOST-HORSES
OF TOÓGAHBOTH

PAST sand-dunes that came on rolling like the surf of a waterless sea, lashed about at the mercy of sudden, howling winds that whipped their crests to a spume; past trees stripped naked until their roots lay in gnarls, and others buried almost to their tips; past clay-formed, painted hills beneath a lurid, dust-smudged sky, they toiled on—father and mother and child. He rode on ahead, his black beard tossed by the gale, his keen eyes glowing with rage. And behind, like furtive shadows, the Indians dogged his steps, falling back when he turned to shoot.

For such horses as he rode had never been seen in the valley of Timbooshah. Behind them there was loot, wagonloads for the taking; but here were four horses that could run like the wind, and their hides were yellow as gold. But, though his eyes gleamed vengefully, Randolph Morgan took no thought of the savages skulking behind. They were no more than the foxes who watched him from the hill-tops. Another enemy was clutching at his throat.

Green trees rose up to mock him, there was rank grass on the flats; but water there was none and the baby at breast cried fretfully and beat her hands. A great valley opened before them, walled in by shadowy mountains which caught the last rays of the sun. But where in all that vastness was there a spring to quench their thirst, a water-hole not poisoned with salts? A dim trail led on along the base of the eastern hills, where wild burros had padded out a path. But where did these asses of the desert drink, and how could they find water at night?

Darkness came, and the man bowed his head to the saddle-horn, the cries of the baby were stilled. Then the bridle-rein fell slack and Selim, son of the desert, snuffed the wind and turned to the east. A range of mountains towered above them, huge and sinister in the dark, and a coyote set up his yell; but the salt-caked floor of the valley had changed to clean sand and the mesquite trees rose up in thickets. The narrow trail that Selim followed turned into another and another until a path, broad and plain, led straight to a trampled hole, pawed deep in a grass-grown flat.

Selim nosed in and sipped, then he drank deep and sighed and Morgan awoke with a start. In his ears was the gurgle of water, the splash of horses pawing mud as they struggled into the hole below. He fought his way among them, saving the last muddy water for his wife and the white-faced child. And then, digging deeper, he let the horses drink their fill before he picketed them out for the night.

Beneath the shelter of a huge mesquite the little family slept, too weary even to think of the prowling Indian forms which had dogged their footsteps at dusk. Dawn found them still sleeping when, with a sudden rush of hoofs, Selim and Neysa burst upon them and a stampede of horses swept past. An Indian warwhoop rent the air and the two fillies were gone, before Morgan could leap to his feet. But Selim stood beside him, tense and eager and trembling to go, and with a curse the man leapt on his back and went whirling down the wind after his foes.

Across the flats like a fury he bore down on the fleeing Indians, who scattered at his impetuous attack. His yellow mount seemed almost to fly as, striking the playa of a dry lake, he galloped down upon them with long strides. Then Morgan's pistol came out and at the first loud report an Indian warrior toppled from his horse. The two fillies were left behind, unnoticed, while the swift yellow stallion skimmed the lake-bed like a swallow and the pistol spoke again. Another warrior, run down, went off into the dirt with a bullet-hole through his back; but with a pitiless hate the black-bearded man turned and went whipping after the rest of the band.

For an hour, while the stolen fillies stood staring, Randolph Morgan chased and shot until the last of his enemies had disappeared in the haze. Then, with both pistols empty, he rode back to camp, his eyes wild with a stern, killing rage. Beaten and thwarted at every point he had turned upon the Indians with the pent-up hate of a madman, and as he looked back down the valley where the looted wagon train lay he called a feud on all mankind.

For a year, striving always to lose himself in the wilderness, yet conscious of his enemies in pursuit; he had pressed on into the West until in desperation he had entered this Valley of Death. The men he had followed had perished ignobly, giving the valley its tragic name; and to the world he too was dead. He turned his eyes to a deep canyon in the range of mountains above him, mountains that towered like a wall in the solitude of the desert yet opened one knife-like fissure to his gaze.

As the sun like a ball of fire rose blazing above the mountain a man and woman and child passed through the knife-gash entrance to Tíngahnee, the Valley of Caves. In the lead paced Selim, his nose to the ground, following the scent of the wary mountain sheep; and at the end of the trail he led the way to a boiling spring, that bubbled up and was lost in the sand. Along the canyon walls were deep caves, their sides blackened by many fires; but never again would the renegade Shoshones use the grinding-holes of Poch Tiṅgahnee. Randolph Morgan had taken it for his own.

Never again, while he lived, would the Indian women come trooping to pick the mesquite beans from the trees. The Shoshone hunters would go elsewhere to kill their mountain sheep, for a devil had taken possession of Cave Canyon. He was seen on the high cliffs that overlooked Toógahboth, the Night Water where the fugitives had camped—a tall man with a white beard, a man who waved his arms and cursed until they fled from Night Water, too.

Years passed and the high mountain where Randolph Morgan hid was called Enúpi Gai, Devils Mountain. In the shadow of the gateway that led up to the boiling spring, where before the Shoshones had camped, there lingered a presence which leapt out at them yelling and chased them across the flats. It was the devil in the form of a man, and they shunned the whole valley below.

At Esahbwoó, where the white people had been poisoned and died, the heavy wagons warped to pieces in the parching desert air and were buried beneath the sands. Nothing remained to tell the story of how they met their death and no more wagon trains came that way. Only prospectors, seeking gold, and outlaws with stolen horses, and fugitives who looked behind as they fled. Mines were found, and men rushed in; but they closed down and the miners left, and once more the Valley of Death lay silent and empty while the winds blew the sand to and fro.

Then an Indian, traveling at night, stopped at Toógahboth for water; and on the playa of the dry lake he beheld four golden horses, running and playing together in the moonlight. They were horses such as no one had ever seen before, with slender legs and high-crested necks, and they ran as no earthly horses can run. Their speed was like an arrow and in the morning when they had vanished there were no tracks on the smooth, dry lake. But the old men remembered the white man with the beard—and the number of his horses was four.

A horse-hunter from Nevada came and camped at Night Water, for the fame of the ghost-horses had spread; but only wild burros wandered into his trap and he rode away in disgust. Many years passed by before the horses were seen again, racing and gambolling by the light of the moon. But when the white men came they found nothing but burros—only Indians could see the Golden Horses of Toógahboth. They ran too fast for earthly steeds—and when the moon was bright a ghost maiden rode with them, back and forth across the lake.

She was of more than mortal beauty, with golden hair like the horses' manes, and when they played on the smooth playa she leapt from horse to horse—and with her ran two sacred foxes. They leapt up at the horses' heads and all played together, until suddenly in the moonlight they vanished from sight and no one could find even a track. Horse-hunters lay, in wait, but the ghostly steeds avoided them; until at last only the Indians kept the story alive of the moon-maiden and her magic mounts. So for twenty years they played and never felt the catch-rope—and then Horse-Ketchum came.

CHAPTER III

MORMON LAKE

THE twenty years brought their changes, not all for the best, but the country to the east settled up. And at Mormon Lake, over the mountains from Death Valley, a store and saloon had been built. A cold, wintry wind, springing up with the dawn, rattling the slats on Bodie's Bar; and four gaunt ponies, tied fast to the horse-rack, bowed their heads to meet the blast. The sore-eyed Indian dogs crept under the house; while, within, the guttering candles still burned on the table and the all-night poker-game dragged on.

Huge and dominant, with bleak blue eyes that followed every flip of a card, Val Bodie sat stripped to his undershirt and overalls, from the band of which a pistol-butt peeped out. Sleeping or waking, no man in fifteen years had caught Bodie without his gun, and he sat with his back to the wall.

Across the table, the mark of the wolf on his face, Hank Boots crouched down behind his hand and thrust out a stack of chips, while his lips drew back in a snarl.

"Win that," he said, "and I'll buy the drinks and quit. By gad, it's almost day."

He glanced at the window where a pale streak of light was struggling through the pane, and for a moment his eyes shifted to three forms on the floor, where his half-breed sons slept like the dead.

"Win that stack and you've got me broke," he added. And Val Bodie spread out his hand.

"You're broke, then," he answered. "But the drinks are on the house. Git up, boys—your daddy is skinned."

"Skinned is right," grumbled Boots as he rose to his full height and stretched his long, gangling arms.

"Well, you asked for it, didn't you?" spoke up Bodie sharply. "Better keep a civil tongue in your head."

"I asked to play a game," returned Boots with an evil smile. "But hell—you *always* win."

"Of course I win!" boasted Bodie. "I'm a man with a head. Never seen the yap yet that could beat me. Here, take a drink of this and get the cobwebs out of your brain—betting your pile on aces and tens!"

He snorted contemptuously and thumped a bottle on the bar and as the three sullen half-breeds lined up for their drink he looked them over intolerantly.

"Every man to his own trade," he said at last. "You boys drift now, and steal some more cows."

"You buy 'em!" retorted Big John Boots. And Bodie nodded insolently.

"Sure," he said. "Every man to his trade. I buy 'em because I know how to sell 'em."

"You know how to stealum, too," muttered the breed. Then Grif Boots took up the tale.

He was tall and Indian black, with glittering eyes that mirrored a settled discontent, and he shifted the gun in his belt.

"We ride long time," he complained. "What's use go stealum cows? Me lay down, go to sleep. Wake up broke—what's use? Me go stealum cow—myself!"

"Yes, and you'll wake up in jail!" answered Val Bodie shortly. "What *you* got to say about it, Pete?"

He turned to the youngest Boots, a boy hardly grown but with a tough, reckless cast of countenance. "Everybody else is belly-aching— what've *you* got to say? You want to steal cows for yourself?"

"Nope. Stealum horses," responded Pete succinctly and Bodie burst into a roar.

"That's a good one!" he laughed. "Have another drink, kid—you've got all the brains in the family. Have another one, boys, and let Pete do your thinking. I'm going out to feed my horse."

21

He set the bottle on the bar and strode out the door and Hank Boots rolled his eyes at his sons. His glance swept the half-empty shelves and he reached over deftly and filched a sack of tobacco. Then, rolling a cigarette, he lounged out the door and sat down to smoke in the sun.

From a corral behind the store eager horses looked out and whinnied as Bodie threw down some hay, but after he had fed them he turned to a closed shed and poured out a feed of grain. Boots watched him and grunted as with purposeful care he rubbed down a clean-limbed mare. Next to whisky and women, Val Bodie loved a race-horse; and this mare, no matter how, had been brought from Missouri to gratify his craving for speed.

"How's that for a horse, boys?" he shouted boastfully as he led the strange mare down to drink. "She's a thoroughbred, I tell ye—watch them legs, when she steps! She cost me a heap of money."

He watched as with dainty grace she bowed her head to the tepid spring and snorted at the alkali smell.

"Oh, she's a lady!" he said. "She's accustomed to the best. And the best ain't none too good for her. While you boys were away I took her over to Pahrump and beat every race-horse in town. They've got some good ones over there now— them gamblers and saloon-keepers are taking in gold, hand over fist. But Fly run away from 'em as if they'd been staked and I came back with a roll."

He slapped his pocket significantly but as the Boots boys exchanged glances he slapped again—at his six-shooter. And they slumped back in baffled discontent. Valentine Bodie was rich—he always had money—but he had killed several men and had served, so it was said, with the Avenging Angels, or Danites.

Hank Boots grunted again and went over to the Indian camp, set back among a grove of huge mesquites. His boys followed behind him, their guns heavy on their hips, their eyes searching the brush houses warily; and as they sat down by the fire the Piutes gave them food, for Boots and his sons were their kin. Smoke rose from the big adobe where Bodie lived with his squaw, breakfast was served and the master came out. But now he carried a riding-saddle and, with his half-grown boy behind him, he led Fly to the edge of the lake.

Mormon Lake it was called, in grim mockery of its dryness, for the clay lake-bed was as dry and smooth as a pavement, as clean and hard-tamped as a race-track. But as Bodie mounted his son and prepared to start him on his canter there was a yell from the dog-pack by the store and the Indians rushed out to look. Over the trail from Death Valley a lone man came striding in, driving two burros heavily loaded with ore-sacks, and Bodie made a run for the store.

"Boys," he announced to the apathetic Boots

family, "here comes Frying-pan George again. I thought you said he was dead?"

"Well, we figgered he was dead," defended Hank Boots lamely. "Follered his tracks plumb out into them sand-hills. Last we seen they was running in circles."

"He fooled you, the old walloper!" declared Val Bodie savagely. "Can't you fellers keep up with a crazy man? He's loco as hell, but he's got a mine somewhere, and this time you follow him to it. What the devil do I feed you for, and keep you in whisky, if you can't turn a trick like that?"

Hank Boots rose up and squinted down his eyes as he surveyed old Frying-pan George. His long, white hair was wrapped up in a red bandanna, which was tucked up beneath his hat, and he stepped forward jauntily in his buckskin pants and moccasins, carrying a rifle across his arm. Two pistols hung on his hips and at sight of his black beard the Piutes broke for the hills.

"You'd better run!" he yelled after them. "I'll kill every one of you. I'll kill 'em all—the lice and the nits!" And he waved his arms threateningly at the crowd.

"Yes, and he will," spoke up Hank Boots. "I know that old devil. And he'll shoot down any man that trails him."

"Heh, scairt a'ready," jeered Bodie. "He don't look bad to me. Look at them sooty-black whiskers, where he's rubbed 'em with the bottom of a frying-pan. He must have an eye out for squaws."

"He's got a woman, somewhere," spoke up Big John Boots. "Always takes home a lot of calico."

"Are *you* afraid of him, too?" demanded Bodie. "Can't *you* trail him up, when he goes? Your old dad here is scairt of his shadow."

"What you pay me?" asked Big John bluntly, and Bodie grabbed him by the shoulder.

"You take me to his mine and I'll make you rich!" he hissed. "Git him drunk, if you can, but trail him! And humor him, boys—he's crazy. All I want now is a look into them sacks."

He laid aside his rifle, which he had grabbed from the store, and walked out to meet his visitor.

"Hello there, George!" he hailed. "I thought you was dead. What you got in them ore-sacks, George?"

Frying-pan George halted his burros and stood glaring at Hank Boots, who peeled his lip back in a scared, wolfish snarl.

"So you're here!" boomed out the prospector, "you Mormon-faced hound! You and your lousy, half-Injun brats! You followed me, when I left here before. But I warn you, right now, the next time you do it, I'll shoot. A squaw-man more or less is nothing to me. So look out or I'll pot you, sure."

He ran his eyes over the crowd and turned back to Bodie, who was regarding him with a placating smile.

25

"I've got ore in those sacks, sir! Ore!" he roared. "Are you willing to pay a fair price?"

"I'll pay you well!" promised the store-keeper eagerly. And without another word Frying-pan George dumped his packs on the ground.

Bodie cut the first sack open greedily and grabbed out a chunk of ore.

"My God!" he exclaimed, "it's rotten with gold. Where do you get all this metal, George?"

"Never mind!" replied Frying-pan bitingly. "All I wish is a price on my ore. Otherwise I'll hit the trail for Pahrump."

"I'll give you six hundred dollars a sack," offered Bodie after a hasty inspection of the ore-bags. "That's a whole lot of money, George."

"It's nothing," declared Frying-Pan, "compared to what the ore is worth. But what could I expect from a renegade Danite, that makes his living by robbing prospectors?"

He whipped out a buckskin thong and began tying up the opened sacks, and Bodie snatched out another piece of ore.

"By grab, boys, that's rich!" he cried admiringly. "Richest gold-ore I ever saw. What's the chance of getting some more, George? I'll give you a thousand dollars a sack for all you bring in. Come on, George—that's lo-ots of money!"

"You ignorant Jack-Mormon!" burst out Frying-pan indignantly, curling up the blackened ends of his beard, "what the devil do *you* know about

26

money? I've handled more in one day than you've seen in a lifetime. I'll have you understand, sir, I'm a gentleman!"

"Sure, sure!" agreed Bodie, "I've seen gentlemen before. And one thing—they never haggled about the price. It's nothing to you, anyway, more than to buy a little grub, and maybe some powder and calico."

"Well, take it!" snapped Frying-pan, "and give me a few necessities, so I can quit this scurvy crew. But put my money in my hand first, before I darken your doorway—four thousand dollars, in gold."

"I'll go get it," promised Bodie, sweating. "But what's your hurry, George? Long time me no see you—come in and have a drink on the house. I've got a new barrel, of the best."

"I never drink," stated Frying-pan, "except with friends. So count out my money and fill this bill of goods. Go away, sir!" And he kicked at a dog.

He stood in the open, muttering angrily to himself as he scanned the low hills to the north; and the Piutes from their hiding-places gazed down at him in terror, while the Boots boys slunk back out of sight. Every Indian, in his presence, felt the imminence of sudden death, for his eyes were crazy with hate. He waited while Bodie brought his payment in gold and stowed his numerous purchases in sacks; but to all his remarks he returned a hostile stare, meanwhile muttering contemptuously in his beard.

The dogs circled him, far away, as if scenting his malevolence and his ever-willing readiness to kill; but as he packed his burros to go they turned their eyes to the northern pass and set up a wild, warning yell. An Indian was topping the ridge, followed by two close-packed mules, and a white man who rode forward to take the lead; but Frying-pan saw only the Indian.

"As I live!" he cursed. "A murdering Shooshonnie. I'd like to kill the last one in the world!"

He stood glaring as they dipped down among the trees, and Bodie spoke to him soothingly.

"That's Captain Jack," he said. "He lives with the Piutes. And he's bringing in a white man that maybe wants to trade, so you'd better leave him alone."

But Frying-pan stood erect, his gun ready to shoot, and Bodie shrugged his shoulders. Captain Jack was no friend of his. The thing that caught his eye was a horse that the stranger led, a creature so deformed that it was almost a humpback, with low withers and a huge, rounded rump. But on its back was a light, English riding-pad, and Bodie looked the cowboy over shrewdly.

He was a tall and slender youth, with black hair and keen dark eyes and an air of braggartly confidence. Yet from the excellence of his rigging and the way he sat his horse it was evident that he knew his way around. He glanced back casually as

Captain Jack ducked in behind him; but though Frying-pan George held his rifle full upon him he did not break his pace.

"Git away from that Injun!" shouted Frying-pan harshly. "He's a cussed Shooshonnie and, by the gods, I'm going to kill him. They're nothing but a bunch of murderers!"

"That's all right," smiled the stranger, "but don't you shoot my Indian. I've hired Captain Jack to take me to a gold-mine, and he can't very well do it if he's dead."

"He's just luring you out into the desert, where he can kill you for your outfit!" charged Frying-pan George vindictively. "I know the whole murderous breed!"

"All the same, you let him live," replied the cowboy evenly. "Because he's a damned good horse-hunter, to boot."

He turned to nod approvingly at the square-shouldered Shoshone, whose sun-blackened countenance had turned ashy, and Bodie stepped into the breach.

"Hello, Jack," he greeted, advancing close enough to Frying-pan to strike up his gun-barrel if necessary. "What the hell are you doing, back here? Old Eatum-up Jake will kill you."

"Me bringum back Hiko man," explained Happy Jack brokenly. "Maybeso findum Breyfogle Mine."

"Find nothing!" snorted Bodie. "Them

Shooshonnies will sure git you, for stealing Eatum-up's gal."

He stepped up closer, and while the cowboy watched Frying-pan he spoke a few words to Jack.

"No!" responded the Indian stubbornly. "Me no run. My boss, she heap brave man."

"That so?" inquired Bodie, glancing fleeringly at the stranger. "What name she got, Jack? Hey?"

"Name—Horse-Ketchum!" answered Happy Jack proudly. "Ketchum wild horse—Sundown Lake."

"The-e—hell!" laughed Bodie. "What you think of that, George? This hombre here is out ketching wild horses. He's got one already. Look at that!"

He jerked a derisive thumb towards the hump-backed led-horse and Frying-pan set down his gun.

"Well," he observed, ignoring Captain Jack and studying the points of the horse, "that ain't the worst horse in the world. Did you find him running wild, my friend?"

"Sure did," nodded Horse-Ketchum. "He's the pick of four hundred that I rounded up at Sundown Lake. No fooling—that horse can run!"

"Yes, and so can that dog!" scoffed Bodie, making a kick at an Indian cur. "W'y, my Lord, stranger, what the devil do you mean, leading him 'round with that pad on his back?"

"I mean," came back Horse-Ketchum, "that old High Behind here can outrun any horse in Nevada, for dollars, dimes or doughnuts."

"You want a race?" barked Bodie eagerly.

"Suit yourself," answered Horse-Ketchum lightly. "Only after I win I don't want any dispute—the first man across the line gets the dough."

"What—with that horse?" laughed Bodie, putting his hands on his hips and walking around High Behind incredulously. "Well, if he ain't sired by Star Plug, out of Battle-Axe, then I sure miss my guess."

"That's all right," returned Horse-Ketchum. "I heard you had a fast mare, so I came down to match a race. Put up or shut up—here's nine hundred dollars that I won in Virginia City."

"You want to *race* me?" shrilled Bodie. "That scrub against Fly? Lemme see if that money is good!"

He snatched the ten-dollar bill that Horse-Ketchum handed him and held it against the sun.

"You're on," he said. "For nine hundred dollars. And George, I'm sure glad you didn't kill Captain Jack or you'd've beat me out of this stake."

CHAPTER IV

THE RACE

THE broad playa of Mormon Lake was a race-track par excellence—so perfect in its smooth hardness, with just a trace of give, that nature could do no more. The horse that could trot out

31

between the stakes of Bodie's straight-away and not break into a lope must be poor and spiritless indeed; but when Johnny Lightfoot—Indian name, Horse-Ketchum—rode High Behind up to the scratch he plodded along at a walk. Val Bodie followed behind him, watching the action of his legs, the muscle-bound rise of his rump, and at the end he burst out laughing.

"Stranger," he said, with a wink at his men and a knowing leer at Frying-pan, "that animile is new in these parts. I've heerd of this here High Behind that inhabits the mountain fastnesses and leaps from crag to crag like a goat, but I've never seen one down on the plains. Now yonder is a sure-enough horse!"

He waved his hand proudly at the dainty mare as she warmed up across the flat, but Horse-Ketchum only grunted.

"A gen-u-wine horse," repeated Bodie, "and not a dee-formed goat. I'd sure like to double that bet!"

"Don't be too damned confident," observed Frying-pan George, squinting his eyes at the humped-back horse. "That nag has got some points."

"Yes, and so has a billy-goat," answered Bodie, rubbing it in. "All this one lacks is the horns. Why don't you bet some of your money if you think he's got a chance? Come on—make a flash—be a sport!"

"I wouldn't bet on a scrub race—and a crooked one, at that," Frying-pan George responded, scathingly.

"Then *you*, stranger," persisted Bodie, riding up beside Horse-Ketchum. "Is that all the money you've got? Well, anything else—that's a nice pair of spurs. I'll lay you fifty dollars against your saddle."

Johnny Lightfoot shrugged thoughtfully and reached down into his pocket. But he brought his hand out empty.

"All I've got," he said at last, "is a little piece of rock that I won from a Virginia City bar-keep. A piece of the original Breyfogle ore—it cost me three hundred dollars. I'll throw it in the hat for five."

"You have!" exclaimed Bodie eagerly, and turned to glance at Hank Boots. "Lemme see it!" he demanded craftily. "How do you know it's the genuine Breyfogle?"

"Because this bar-keeper bought it from Breyfogle himself when he came back out of Death Valley. He put it up for the drinks."

"Well, lemme see it!" insisted Bodie. "And if I think it's worth the price—"

"You win this race," said Horse-Ketchum, "and the rock is yours. You lose and you don't get a look. I'm hunting for that mine, myself."

"Hoo, hoo!" mocked the store-keeper. "Out looking for the Breyfogle, like all these other Smart Ellicks. Did you ever think, Pardner, that if

33

that mine was really here, some of us old-timers would've found it?"

"You can't find a mine, sitting around a saloon," observed Johnny Lightfoot oracularly. And Frying-pan George laughed heartily. His early antipathy towards Captain Jack's protector had changed to a fatherly tolerance which almost verged upon approval.

"Well, I'll go you," agreed Bodie, "for five hundred dollars. But who's going to hold the stakes?"

"Give 'em to Jack," suggested Johnny. "He's seen the rock already." And he brought it out, wrapped up in a handkerchief.

"No, I know that danged Injun," spoke up Bodie brutally. "Any buck that will steal a woman will steal the stakes—or anything else. Let's ask Mr. Boots here to serve."

"You do," cut in Frying-pan, "and you'll have a thorough-paced scoundrel, that stands in, hand and glove, with Val Bodie."

"Well, in that case," grinned Johnny, handing over the rock, "I'll just ask you to be the stake-holder, my friend."

"Very well, sir," beamed Frying-pan, "and you have my word, as a gentleman, that no one shall see this ore. You're a new man in these parts, so I might as well tell you that you've fallen into a den of thieves. There isn't a man here that wouldn't kill you for your winnings, or hold out the stakes if you won. You can govern yourself accordingly."

"I'll just put this gun where I can find it, then," answered Horse-Ketchum, after a glance at Val Bodie and his gang. And he tucked a pistol under his belt. Then, still smiling serenely, he dropped off his horse and began to rub High Behind down.

"Why don't you give him a little run and kinder warm him up?" suggested Bodie, after waiting around uneasily for the start.

"That ain't my system," responded Lightfoot shortly. "How far do you want to run?"

"Quarter-mile," announced Bodie. "That's Fly's regular distance. And we'll start at the drop of the hat."

"Suits me," agreed Johnny. "The stake-holder is the judge and no fouls allowed. The first man across the line wins."

"See here!" demanded the store-keeper, arrogantly, "what shenanigan are you up to, Mister? Do you figure on fouling my mare? I'll just warn you, right now, you lay a hand or a whip on Fly and I'll fill you full of lead!"

"All right," agreed Horse-Ketchum, "and the same goes for High Behind. So lay off—and keep away from that home-stretch."

He handed his hat to Captain Jack, with some muttered instructions, and swung up on his humped-back horse. And suddenly the spiritless steed broke into an effortless canter which made Bodie stop and stare. With his ewe-neck craned and his head thrust awkwardly out he looked more like a camel than a horse, but in some miraculous way he got over the ground and Val Bodie made a grab for Pete Boots.

"Git that burro down here," he whispered, "and git him here quick. This son-of-a-goat can run."

Strange as it seemed in retrospect, every man there present suddenly realized that High Behind had speed. That great rump which so deformed him was a mountain of bulging muscles which made him bounce like a rubber ball. Johnny rode him down the track to the scratch; then back again, running, towards the finish, where Bodie and his minions stood staring.

"What's the idea," demanded Johnny, "in setting all these posts along the track? Why don't we pull this off in the open?"

"Oh, them's jest to keep the Injuns off the track," the saloon-keeper answered glibly. "They're hell to crowd in on the finish."

"Well, don't *you* do it," warned Horse-Ketchum, "or I'll ride plumb over you. I may look easy, but I'm here to win this race—so don't pull any crooked stuff, whatever!"

"The same to you, Mister!" answered Val Bodie insolently. "You act pretty fresh, for a kid."

"I run my horse on the square," retorted Lightfoot. "And I'd advise you to do the same. Otherwise we're liable to have trouble."

He turned his horse in his tracks and trotted off down the course, but as he lined up at scratch he saw Pete Boots on a burro, flogging recklessly out from the store. Frying-pan George had his hat held high in the air, and Fly's jockey was whirling her trickily in an effort to beat the game. But the hat did not drop and the half-breed came jouncing back to where High Behind stood fretting.

Once more the hat went up and the next instant it dropped. Fly was caught fighting her head, and with a single mighty bound High Behind jumped out into the lead. Horse-Ketchum bent low and shot his mount down the track at a pace that increased with every stride. The awkward ewe-necked creature became suddenly transformed into a living embodiment of speed. His long hind-legs propelled him like a giant kangaroo and with each sweeping hop he pulled away from the high-bred Fly as if she were only a scrub.

The half-breed boy pulled his whip and laid it across her rump in a frantic tattoo of blows. But High Behind raced on, a good four lengths ahead, and Horse-Ketchum saw the money in his hat. Before him in a blur there rose the crowd at the finish, and the line of narrowing mesquite posts flitting past; and then, moving slowly, a burro shuffled out, dragging a heavy rope across his path.

It was the same big burro that he had seen galloping out as he lined up to start the race, and Horse-Ketchum sensed a trap. The next instant he

37

was into it, for Hank Boots had sprung out and laid hold of the dragging rope. The burro set back obstinately at the tug of the rope, effectively blocking the track, and Fly was dashing up behind. If Johnny slowed down she would pass him on the run—when the rope was opportunely dropped flat—and beat him out at the finish.

A shout of warning rose up and men rushed to seize the rope, while Bodie ran out, waving his arms. But though he waved, Horse-Ketchum did not check his racer's speed—the first man across the line won. Straight at the balky burro he headed his mount and Bodie dodged back just in time. High Behind broke his stride and gathered his feet like a rabbit. Then with a high, graceful leap he jumped clear over the burro and went pelting down the track to victory.

With one resistless tug Val Bodie and his gang snaked the burro clear off the track, but their desperate ruse had failed and Fly came dashing in, a beaten and disheartened horse. High Behind had won the race—but could his master collect the stakes? Horse-Ketchum reined back and drew his gun.

CHAPTER V

A FREE COUNTRY

THERE was a rush toward the stake-holder as Horse-Ketchum turned back to claim the pile of money he had won. All cursing at once, Val Bodie and his gang had swarmed in to protest the race; and with his black hair flying Johnny Lightfoot split the wind to get in before the stakes were lost. Straight at the crowd he rode and as they scattered before his charge he dropped off and stood, gun in hand.

"I claim that race!" he said, turning to Frying-pan George. "You know the rules—the first man in!"

"That's right," agreed Frying-pan, reaching down into his hat. "Here's your money—and here's your rock."

"Much obliged," mumbled Johnny, stuffing the stakes into his pocket as he faced the surly crowd. "And now, you dirty whelps, you can all go to hell—and take your trick burro with you."

"That was just a little accident," explained Bodie briskly. "But there's one thing I want cleared up. A race is a race, and my nine hundred is gone. But I put up five hundred dollars against a rock I've never seen, and I claim you won it on nothing. It's all right for you to say that it's Breyfogle ore, but I'd just like to *see* that rock!"

"You'll see nothing!" declared Horse-Ketchum. "Because I told you at the start—"

"Now here," broke in Bodie, "I'm a peaceable man but, by the gods, this is going too far. Pulling a gun won't get you nowhere when you're talking to me—I've tamed worse men than you are. All I want is to know that you've got such a rock and that it's the genuine Breyfogle ore."

"That's right, and that's fair!" spoke up Hank Boots from behind him. "And if it comes to a fight—count me in!"

He stepped up beside his boss, and as his sons lined up behind him, Horse-Ketchum put up his gun.

"Well—hell," he grumbled, "I'm not hunting for trouble. But suppose I show you this rock—who's going to decide whether or not it's the genuine ore?"

"I can do that, gentlemen!" broke in Frying-pan pompously. "I'm familiar with the Breyfogle rock. But if once Val Bodie gets his hands on that specimen—"

"Then take it!" offered Johnny impulsively.

He handed over the knotted handkerchief and Frying-pan opened it grimly, shielding the ore in his fists as he gazed. For a moment he stood blinking—then with a slow, strange smile he wrapped it up, in the cloth.

"Young man," he said, "that's the genuine Breyfogle. But you might as well go back where you came from. Because, gentlemen, I brought four sacks of that same, identical ore and sold it at the store, this morning."

"Like hell you did!" jeered Bodie. And then with a lightning slap he knocked the handkerchief out of his hand. But as he stooped to snatch it up Horse-Ketchum stamped down on it, and Frying-pan whipped out his guns.

"You keep back!" he ordered, as Lightfoot grabbed the rock and rammed it into his pocket. "Keep back—and listen to me. There's no use fighting over this Breyfogle ore, because I've had the mine staked for years. And another thing, gentlemen—remember what I told you! Don't any of you whelps try to follow me!"

He backed off towards the store, a pistol in each hand, his eyes on the men who, like a pack of wolves, were resolute to pull him down. Val Bodie was in the lead, and behind him Hank Boots with his band of half-breed sons—and suddenly their craven fear was gone. The Breyfogle Mine was the greatest treasure that Death Valley held hid from mankind. The man who first discovered it had carried out enough ore to set the whole country gold-mad. Expedition after expedition had started back under his leadership, but each time he approached the scene of his early sufferings the madness which had possessed him returned.

Taken captive by the Indians, he had wandered from place to place; until at last, finding the gold, he had used his shoes for canteens and fled bare-footed across the desert. Leaving Death Valley at night he had passed two high buttes, below which were three white spots, like springs. At Hole-in-the-Rock he had drunk and passed on; until at daylight, topping a pass, he had discovered the seep of water still known as Daylight Spring. Here he put on his shoes and wandered far to the south and east, trailed for days by the curious Piutes who struck him down at last for his huge "moccasins."

But the gold they did not take and emigrants, passing by, found him wounded and out of his head. Nor could he say where he had got the ore. He maundered of hidden springs, of a partner killed by Indians, of himself taken captive and ridden like a horse by a band of renegade Shoshones. He remembered the two buttes, set at the entrance to the canyon at whose head he had found Daylight Spring, and the three white spots, like the seep of alkali springs, which he had seen near their base from the peaks. But whence the gold had come he could never tell, for the stone war-club of a Piute had knocked out of his head the one memory that men sought most.

Fifteen years and more had passed and now at Bodie's Store a flash of the elusive secret had been revealed. Two men, riding in, had brought—one a piece of the ore, another four sacks from its source. But whence came this gold that Frying-pan George packed in to trade for supplies at the store? And

42

were the two pieces of ore really the same? One mystery succeeded another, for no man at Mormon Lake had seen Horse-Ketchum's rock. All they had was the word of a half-crazy prospector that his ore and the Breyfogle were identical. But Val Bodie had them both in his power.

Plodding out through the gap that led to Daylight Pass and the arid waste of Death Valley beyond, Frying-pan George drove his burros with the load of powder and supplies for which he had bartered his gold. He was keen and wary now, with his rifle across his arm, looking back often and shouting shrill threats. But the road he must follow led off across a desert that stretched smooth to Death Valley's rim. On that broad, level plain, with the greasewood so evenly spaced that it looked like a planted field, not even a jack-rabbit could hide. And his burros were slow—George would keep.

With his winnings in his pockets and Captain Jack behind, Horse-Ketchum had swung off into the Pahrump trail that led to the east and south. But the open, barren desert offered no hiding-place for him and Val Bodie came hot on his trail. Horse-Ketchum looked back, and unslung his rifle which he carried beneath his knee, for trouble was no novelty to him. In fact he rather sought it, as a moth seeks the flame—and so far his wings were unsinged.

"Go back!" he signaled, placing a bullet in front of Bodie. And the bad-man came to a halt. Then he raised his hand in the peace-sign, waved his fighting men back, and rode out across the flat for a talk.

"Now, here," he began, as they met in the open, "I can't stop to monkey around with a kid like you—I want to see that rock."

He had mounted a big roan, slung a gun-belt around his waist and a rifle scabbard on his saddle. Down the trail behind him on their desert-toughened ponies Hank Boots and his sons sat watching them intently, ready to ride in if a battle sprang up. But Horse-Ketchum did not flinch.

"Say," he mocked, "do you own this country? I've got a use for that specimen, myself."

"Well, you try to find the Breyfogle—or let me ketch you trailing George—and I'll damn soon show you what's what. I may not own the country, but I come pretty near running it. And you give me a little more of your lip and I'll sure plant you where you won't grow."

"I was just going to say," went on Horse-Ketchum imperturbably, "that I'm free, white and twenty-one and I'll do what I dodram please."

"Yes—I've heard that before," nodded Bodie, "from a damn-sight better fighting man than you are. But I happen to be in a hurry right now—how much do you want for that rock?"

"I've got all the money I need," grinned Lightfoot. "What you think of old High Behind, now?"

"I'll be riding him in a month," retorted Bodie. "Soon as I get old George off my hands. He's a good horse and I need him—and while we're on the subject, what's that Injun, Captain Jack, been telling you? I knew danged well, the minute I seen him, he was bringing you in here either to hunt for the Breyfogle or to ketch them wild horses at Night Water."

"That's right," nodded Johnny. "Horse-ketching is my business. What's the matter—isn't this a free country?"

"Well," responded Bodie, "it is and it isn't. I reckon you've never been in here before. Ever hear of Bodie's Danites. It's jest a name, of course— nothing to do with the Mormon Church—but at the same time it covers the case. There ain't much of this country that ain't looked after by some of my riders, and we generally work by night. Kind of Night Riders, you savvy, and our principal occupation is looking after hombres like you. Sometimes we treat 'em easy, like I'm treating you now; and then again, my friend, we treat 'em rough as hell and bury 'em out in some dry-wash."

"Yes, I've heard about that," admitted Horse-Ketchum defiantly, "but Mr. Bodie, you don't look bad to me. And that goes for those half-breeds, too. I've trimmed you on a horse-race and got away with the boodle, and I believe I can do the same with the Breyfogle. That is, if I happen to find it. But I've heard a whole lot about those Death

Valley horses and you can't bluff me out—I'm going."

"You go," blustered Bodie, "and I'll see that you don't come back. There's no law in this country— no sheriffs, no nothing—and what Valentine Bodie says, goes! Them horses are mine. I've been over and seen 'em and I claim 'em by right of discovery. I sent plumb back to Missouri to get a horse fast enough to ketch 'em—that's how come I happen to have Fly. I've got Injuns on the lookout for horse-hunters coming through there, with orders to smoke 'em out. And I'll promise you, right now, you'll never get off alive if you try to put a rope on my stock.

"Now that's doing a lot of explaining for a smart Ellick like you, that ought to be handled with a club, but as I said before I'm too busy to monkey with you and so I'm warning you out. Hit that trail there and keep a-going—and don't you come back, because I don't want you around here, at all."

Bodie paused and regarded Horse-Ketchum with a pair of steel-gray eyes that were cold and murderously calm, eyes that opened up unpleasantly, showing too much of the white, eyes that had gazed on dead men and smiled. He was a natural-born killer, but Horse-Ketchum was young and he answered his threats with a smile.

"Well, that's plain, Mr. Bodie," he said. "And next time I see you coming I'll know just exactly what to do. The only trouble is, I'm not used to

46

taking orders from a pot-bellied squaw-man like you. This is a free country, by grab—or if it ain't I'll make it free. And meanwhile, you hit that trail!"

He jerked his thumb towards the road that led back to Mormon Lake and Bodie eyed him dourly.

"All right, Mister," he answered. "I was going back, anyhow, so you can take your hand off of that gun. And don't you never think I'm bluffed. I've got other business on hand—trailing up Frying-pan George. And meanwhile *you* hit the trail. Understand?"

He wheeled his horse with a savage jerk and galloped back towards his men, while Horse-Ketchum regarded him thoughtfully.

"On the prod," he muttered, "as big as a wolf. But I'll buy in on this, all the same."

CHAPTER VI

THE FORBIDDEN WATER-HOLE

FROM the top of a high butte on the Pahrump trail Horse-Ketchum, the trouble-hunter, watched five far-away horsemen riding out towards Daylight Pass. And ahead of them, like a shadow on the face of the desert, he saw through his glasses two burros that plodded west, flogged on by a black-bearded man. He passed up over the high divide and dipped down into Death Valley and the five horsemen suddenly leapt into a lope.

"Come on, Jack," said Horse-Ketchum, "I've got cards in this game. Maybeso we find the Breyfogle Mine."

"Nope—no findum," grunted Captain Jack, his keen eyes still following the chase. "Frying-pan—she crazy. You think she ketchum mine? No good. Me trailum, long time."

Lightfoot laughed at the badly mixed pronouns, but his eyes lighted up at the news.

"Oho!" he exclaimed, "so you've back-tracked George yourself, eh?"

"Long time, me trailum. She shoot like hell. No go to mine—turn back like fox. Every time Injum come—she shootum. Then long time me wait—see George going back. Two burros—plenty gold, like now."

He stopped and chuckled, his strong teeth flashing white against the sunburned blackness of his skin.

"Me follow tracks back," he said. "Findum hole—no gold! Frying-pan stealum gold—then buryum. Bimeby she come back—digum up—tell Bodie ketchum mine."

"I see!" nodded Horse-Ketchum. "But where does he get this ore, then? Maybe you and me can steal a little, too."

"No-o. No good," returned Captain Jack soberly, rubbing a bullet-mark on his neck. "More better ketchum horse."

"What horse?" inquired Horse-Ketchum absently.

"Wild horse!" wheedled Jack. "Good horse—kinder yeller. You think High Behind good horse? You think Fly-horse run fast? *No wano*—me show you *good* horse!"

"In Death Valley?" demanded Horse-Ketchum eagerly. And the Shoshone nodded knowingly.

"Death Valley—upper end. Long time Val Bodie try ketchum."

"Umm!" mumbled Lightfoot, polishing his gun-butt dubiously. "Ain't you scared Mr. Bodie will kill us?"

"Maybeso we kill him," suggested Captain Jack, his crafty eyes gleaming wickedly. "These Shooshonnie horse—no b'long Val Bodie. Death Valley, Shooshonnie country. This side them mountains, all Piute country—savvy? Other side, all belong Shooshonnie."

"Yes, but how about that girl you stole from Eatum-up Jake? Bodie says the Shooshonnies will kill you."

"Nope. No stealum—run away," defended Captain Jack angrily. "Then pretty soon he marry white man. Me no stealum girl. Me good Injun, savvy? You let Shooshonnie kill me?"

"No by grab!" declared Horse-Ketchum. And suddenly Captain Jack smiled.

"You good man," he said. "my friend. You no let nobody kill me, eh? All right—me brave man—big warrior. You come—me show you horse."

"That's a go!" agreed Horse-Ketchum, holding out his hand. And Captain Jack shook it briefly.

"Me show you good horse," he stated. "Too good, these horse. Nobody can ketchum. Maybeso spirit-horse—run fast."

"Let 'em run," boasted Lightfoot. "If I can't ketch 'em with High Behind I'll give you a hundred dollars!"

"*Wano*! Good!" laughed Captain Jack. "Me buy me 'nother squaw. These horse come night-time. No likum sun. You think you ketchum—moonlight?"

"You bet ye!" nodded Johnny. "Ketchum any time."

"Pretty horse!" praised Jack, rolling his eyes ecstatically. "Yeller horse—come play on dry lake. Me watchum long time—ride out—try ropum. No good—run fast, like that."

He clipped one hand across the other in the Indian sign for speed and Horse-Ketchum jerked out his roll.

"Jack!" he said, "you put me and High Behind where we can get a straight run at them horses and I'll give you two hundred dollars. I got plenty— two hundred dollars!"

"Good! Good!" agreed Captain Jack. "Me buy me two squaw." And he laughed as he brought up Johnny's horse.

"You see moon?" he asked, pointing up at a pale crescent in the sky. "Bymeby come down there—

get big. Come full moon—me show you horse."

"All right," replied Lightfoot. "Where you want to go now, Jack? Maybeso Val Bodie kill me."

"Nope. No killum," promised Captain Jack. "We go long ways—come back. Go Death Valley—come back. Val Bodie no seeum—no killum."

"Good enough," agreed Horse-Ketchum. And as he fell in behind him he looked back at Mormon Lake and laughed.

The moon, which was on the wane, rose later and later, to float pale and wan through the sky; until at last it hung at dusk, crystal-clear in the west—a new moon that grew and grew. The next evening it hung higher, an hour above the horizon; and so, night by night, until it rose in the east, huge and yellow in the last rays of the sun.

For two weeks and more they had wandered through desert ranges, losing their tracks on the beds of dry lakes. But as the moon soared high, turning the color of gold, Captain Jack swung back into the north. Traveling trails that only his people knew he headed towards the valley of Timbooshah, and Horse-Ketchum found himself lost. Mountains rose where he expected valleys until at last, mounting a divide, he sensed the great abyss.

They stood at Daylight Pass and below them, lost in moonlight, Death Valley seemed to shimmer and breathe. It lay before them, that mighty chasm where the earth had been rent and then half-healed of its wound. A warm wind came to meet them as they descended into the depths, until suddenly at a black point the great sink appeared, its salt marshes gleaming in the moonlight. But the Indian had wrapped himself in the mantle of silence, and Horse-Ketchum held his peace.

They had entered unaware into an enemy country, where every man's hand was against them. Wandering Piute or vengeful Shoshone or the Night Riders of Val Bodie would alike take up their trail. And when, on the floor of the valley, they encountered the first sand-hills, Captain Jack lost his tracks in the dunes. Then as the mountains to the west cast their moon-shadow upon them he turned and rode to the north.

Rocky washes crossed their path and wide expanses of salt-meadow, where the crusted earth glistened with alkali. Then huge sand-hills, studded with mesquite trees, rose up from the gathering darkness and they struggled through a chaos of dunes. The moon had sunk from sight behind the ramparts of the Panamints; and in the east, above mountains that rose like a wall, there glowed the first light of dawn. They came out on a dry lake-bed and before them, like fleeting shadows, strange creatures wheeled and fled into the night.

"Toógahboth!" muttered the Indian as he reined in his horse. And for a long time they listened in silence to the patter of retreating hoofs. Then, down the wind, there came a loud whistling snort and Horse-Ketchum's heart leapt with joy. Unseen by friend or foe he had reached forbidden Night Water, and the golden horses were there.

CHAPTER VII

INDIAN DEVILS—AND GHOSTS

AT dawn, while their horses drank deep at the water-hole, Captain Jack circled the spring, his head low like a hunting-dog as he read the story written in the sand. Like a guiding automaton his forefinger swung here and there, lingering briefly as he studied out each track; until at last it came to a stop. Daintily stamped in the wet soil was the footprint of a horse, round and firm and exquisitely formed.

"Yeller horse!" he explained, as Horse-Ketchum came. And then he pointed again. Half trampled by other tracks but stabbed deep into the dirt was the mark of an iron-shod hoof.

"Val Bodie!" he pronounced and Horse-Ketchum nodded. His enemy had been there, and gone.

"This bad place," observed Jack uneasily. "Injun devil watchum, too. She live up there—on mountain. Callum Enúpi Gai—my people."

He fixed his beady eyes on the forbidding cliffs of Devil Mountain, and for a long time scanned them, intently. Then he drew back closer behind the shelter of the trees and hastened to lead the animals out of sight. He bored deeper into the thicket of thorny mesquites that flanked the dry lake-bed on the west, and when all were safely hidden he crept to a brushy hillock and once more gazed up at the cliffs.

They rose like the battlements of some mediaeval castle, their striated walls painted black and iron-red, or flecked with strange yellows and chromes. And behind them, deep in shadow, Horse-Ketchum could see a canyon, cut out of the mountain's heart. Only the gash of a narrow gateway made its presence believable, and the wide sluicing flow of the sand-wash, where cloudbursts had belched forth their waste. It was a place easily peopled by the savage imagination with demons which rushed forth to kill.

"Injun devil live up there," croaked Captain Jack at last. "We no lightum fire—she come down—maybe killum. Long time ago killum plenty. Shooshonnies. My people no come here no more."

"What look like—this devil?" inquired Horse-Ketchum indulgently as he trained his powerful glasses on the cliff. "And say, Jack, where are all those horses?"

"All gone," responded the Indian solemnly. "Maybeso moon takum. Yeller horse only come at night. One time me hide here—see spirit-woman ride horse. Me think he drivum away."

"Maybe so," agreed Horse-Ketchum. "Injuns see lots of spirits, eh? You ever see this devil-man, Jack?"

"Me seeum!" asserted Captain Jack positively. "Tall man—long hair. Long whiskers—all white. She see us, she come down—killum. You look long time, top side big canyon-mouth—maybeso you seeum, too."

Lightfoot shifted his glasses to the crags above the gateway; but the great shelves and benches were empty and lifeless, without even a mountain sheep. There was not a tree or bush from the summit of the mountain to the base of the sun-blackened cliffs. All was barren, deserted; and yet as he gazed he too peopled the mountain with ghosts. From the shadow of a rock something rose up and slipped away—perhaps a man or a sheep or a light specter caused by heat, which was making the desert bushes dance.

The sun was over the peaks, pulling them out into strange shapes, distorting the broad valley which lay to the south until it shimmered in the semblance of a lake. As the sand absorbed its rays the mesquite trees seemed to rise, as if floating away into space. Their gnarly tops were pulled up high—the mirage made them islands and their trunks became long, trembly stems. Horse-Ketchum crawled up again when the sun was smiting hot and trained his glasses on the demon-haunted crags; but only an Indian's eyes could see the man-devil, gazing out over his desert domain.

In the breathless silence of midday the valley lay sleeping beneath its blanket of palpitating heat; but as the sun touched the peaks a wind came stealing in, stirring the tops of the limp mesquites. Far away across the flats, where they had been grazing on the sacaton, a line of wild burros headed back towards the water-hole, plodding slowly as if in a muse. But not a horse was in sight and Horse-Ketchum became restless, for he did not believe in ghosts.

If the golden horses of Toógahboth came down at night to drink, and to gambol and play on the lake-bed, his white man's reason told him that they did not come from the moon but from somewhere in that broad expanse. Before the dawn he had heard them as they pattered across the playa, and the wild, whistling snort of the stallion; but at daylight they were gone, as if indeed some ghostly maiden had driven them home to the moon.

At dusk they watered their animals and turned them out to browse on the leaves and beans of the mesquites; while from his pack Horse-Ketchum measured out a feed of grain and fed it to High Behind. Then as darkness came on he rubbed him down and cinched on the saddle and limbered up his throw-rope for the chase. When the moon rose over the mountain, like a globe of sun-kissed gold, he was waiting on the edge of the lake.

Down the wind there came the bedlam of wild

asses braying and the rush of contending jacks as they fought. Then the burros came trooping in, to gather by the water-hole and descend one by one for a drink. Pawing the sand back night by night they had dug a trench so deep that only their rumps remained in sight. Horse-Ketchum thrilled at the thought of some glorious, golden horse, placidly drinking while he made his rush. But the horses of the moon did not come.

Higher and higher it soared, into a sky where the stars faded to nothing before its effulgence. Every tree and twig stood out, and the white playa of the lake stretched before him as clear as day. But it was empty, except for the last of the burros as they plodded towards the salt-flats to feed. Horse-Ketchum felt his senses reel in a species of moon madness as he gazed out over the scene. Upon a night like that he could almost believe in moon-maidens, and flying steeds that no man could rope. But if any horses appeared he was determined to ride out at them and match High Behind's speed against theirs.

There was a whistle, from far away towards Enúpi Gai where the devil lay watching for his prey; and Horse-Ketchum tightened up his cinch. Then as High Behind raised his head and snorted back the challenge he reached up and grabbed his nose. Not six months before, on the playa of Sundown Lake, he too had run free, rejoicing in his speed, until at last he had felt the rope. He was a wild horse still, and only the stout hackamore held him back from a dash into their midst.

They came pattering across the lake, dim forms that glided near as easily as if they rode on a moonbeam. Horse-Ketchum could see their heads as they flung them on high to snuff at the tainted wind. But he had placed himself well, where no scent of his could reach them; and the horses, still snorting, came on. He caught the lines of a crested neck, a small head and a short, straight back as the leading stallion circled close. Then with a shrill, explosive snort he turned and scampered off, golden yellow in the light of the moon.

Horse-Ketchum hid close, twisting the hackamore on High Behind to choke off his answering neighs; and as he saw once more the tossing heads coming close he turned and swung up on his mount. Man and horse alike were trembling now, the horse with eagerness to dash out and join his kind, his rider at the beauty of his prizes. Every line of their trim bodies spoke of symmetry and speed; and their tails, floating behind, stood out straight as tufted arrows. They came galloping, fleet as the wind.

Yet some instinct had taught them to avoid the crescent of trees that surrounded the lake and spring, and as he set himself to go Horse-Ketchum felt misgivings. For the first time he doubted High Behind's speed. Fastest of all wild horses at Sundown Lake, faster even than the thoroughbred

Fly, there was something about the action of these swift, dashing mustangs that told Lightfoot his steed would fail. The horse-band went thundering past him, their manes and tails like wind-tossed plumes; and he drew back, sweating, to wait.

In the open by the water-hole the circling mustangs came to a halt while a beautiful mare, their leader, stepped out from the rest and Lightfoot counted seven more. Eight horses, so clean and perfect that each seemed a replica—and all yellow as gold in the moonlight. She advanced, snuffing the air, turning her head to right and left as if she sensed the hidden horsemen in the brush. But no one dashed out and she stepped down into the trench, bowing her head to the water in the depths.

The others crowded closer, eager to slake their all-day thirst but uneasy within the circle of the trees. Horse-Ketchum made a balk to charge out among them, but thought better of it while yet there was time. Once filled up with water their speed would be cut down by enough, perhaps, to make one his prey. But even when the stallion ventured down into the pit Horse-Ketchum did not shake out his rope. Now, while that proud head was hidden, was the time to make his charge, to stampede the logy herd and capture the leader himself—but Horse-Ketchum had lost his nerve. Something told him that to start was to fail, and he let the golden moment pass.

The stallion backed out swiftly, throwing his

head into the air; then in a senseless stampede, playing and snapping as they ran, they sped out across the lake-bed. Far off to the east they galloped, and Lightfoot thought they were lost until suddenly he heard their swift feet returning. Yet now there was a difference, coming subtly to his ear that was trained to measure such cadences—it seemed as if one of them was ridden.

They loomed up, dim and ghostly in the moonlight, which veiled them with a soft, effulgent glow; and now, a solid troop, they thundered by like charging soldiers and Horse-Ketchum saw the leader wheel and guide. Then as they swung in behind him Lightfoot beheld a woman's form, leaning forward along his neck as she rode. Her hair mingled with his mane, her body seemed part of his; until suddenly she rose up, revealing a face white and ghostly, and golden hair that flowed out behind. Then in a clatter of hoof-beats she was gone.

Horse-Ketchum rubbed his eyes and stared up at the moon, but the memory of that girl-face remained. Then again the hoof-beats came and he gazed out, incredulously, for the ghost-woman was riding, straight up. She rode bareback, graceful and slender, on a mare that caracoled as gently as any in a circus; and as the stallion came rushing past she leapt lightly upon his back, seizing his mane with a swift, triumphant swing. They were off in a galloping circle, leaving the others far behind, and like a man in a dream Horse-Ketchum watched their prankish play as the stallion came cantering back.

But now, running beside her, were two silvery-grey foxes, the black tips of their tails whipping about in the wind as they glided, unseen, over the ground. Except for their black tips they were grey shadows on a grey lake-bed; but as they dashed into the lead they leapt up at the stallion's head, like dogs inviting their master to play.

Horse-Ketchum sat rigid, his useless rope still in his hand, and let the shadowy racers dart by. Here were horses, his eyes told him—the finest in the world—and a woman, more beautiful than he had dreamed. But whence came these foxes, to run and play at the stallion's head? And where had they suddenly gone? He strained his eyes, to pierce the darkness, which no moonlight could quite dispel; and in the distance, moving together, he saw them gallop away until suddenly the night swallowed them up. With a curse he hurled his coil of rope to the ground and turned to find Captain Jack beside him.

"Somebody come!" he stated stolidly, pointing off to the south. And Horse-Ketchum came back to earth. While he, in a sort of dream, had watched the horses on the lake, Captain Jack, ever vigilant, had been searching the night for enemies—for at Night Water no man was their friend.

They took cover, and a single horseman came

trotting out on the playa, as if driving the golden horses into a trap. And suddenly, from the east, a loud yell rent the air and in a stampede the horse herd came back. They were running wildly now, straight out across the lake-bed where nothing could impede their flight; and behind them in a half circle shadowy riders appeared, whipping and spurring to cut them off. The lone rider had checked his steed and as Horse-Ketchum crouched, staring, Captain Jack spoke hoarsely in his ear.

"Val Bodie!" he said. "Ridum Fly-horse." And even as he spoke Bodie charged. Like an arrow the high-bred mare shot out across the lake-bed; while, Bodie, big and burly, shook a loop out of his rope, leaning forward to make his throw. But the mustangs had seen him coming—they swerved sharply to the south—and in a wild clatter of hoofs they raced off through the night, leaving Bodie and his thoroughbred behind.

Horse-Ketchum laughed shortly as he witnessed his rival's defeat. Then Captain Jack took command.

"No ketchum," he said. "We go." And Horse-Ketchum turned reluctantly away.

"All right, Jack," he answered. "But bimeby we come back. And then I'll ketch me—one horse."

CHAPTER VIII

ONE HORSE

WHEN the moon, yellow as gold, sank down in the west and the sun topped the mountains to the east, Horse-Ketchum, still riding, gazed back into the valley where the horses of Toógahboth ran. Val Bodie on his thoroughbred had been left at the start—the horse did not live that could match them—and yet as he gazed he muttered again:

"Some day I'll ketch me—one horse."

Would it be the regal stallion that the moon-girl had seemed to ride, with a mane as yellow as her hair; or the mare who led the race, when the cowboys came charging in and they fled in a wild stampede? Or the filly, as free as air, which had kept its mother's pace, its head and tail lined out straight? There was speed, and grace and beauty—but every one of them possessed it. They were perfect—the finest horses in the world!

Horse-Ketchum's mount was tiring, but Captain Jack spurred on, his dark face grim and set. The pack-mules jerked their heads and lagged as they broke their trot, but the Indian lashed them ruthlessly on. He did not look back, for he knew they would be followed as soon as daylight revealed their tracks. Val Bodie had promised to send them both to hell, and his Night Riders would try to make good.

At noon, from the black peak that guarded a hot spring, they saw the dust of the distant pursuit, and Captain Jack lightened his packs. Horse-Ketchum changed to High Behind and they turned off up a side-canyon that led to the high plains beyond. All day, without pursuers, they fled on to the east; crossing the Grape-vine Mountains and still pressing on until they came to a small, dry lake.

"Me foolum," promised Jack, riding out on its polished surface. And after losing his tracks in circles he turned to the south, doubling back towards Mormon Lake. Not till daylight, if then, would the weary Avengers find the cleverly hid trail they had made. And by then more dry lake-beds would conceal their bold flight, straight back into the lion's den. Only when a pack-mule quit and laid down beneath the lash did the Shoshone seek shelter and camp.

All day they lay in hiding, and the next night, beneath the moon, they circled until they passed Mormon Lake. Then, tirelessly, night after night, Captain Jack lost his trail and rode on, to lose it again.

"Me foolum," he said, grinning, and Horse-Ketchum nodded. And so the moon waxed, and waned. But as it soared once more towards its throne in the east, whence soon it would emerge, a full moon; as it lighted up the dry lakes with unearthly splendor, Horse-Ketchum returned to his dream. On the playa of Toógahboth he saw the horses of the moon, trooping in to slake their thirst at the spring. He saw the stallion, his head erect, his golden mane gleaming, circling the flat while he whistled his alarm. And then the mare, her slender legs all set to wheel and run, walking in on the pawed-out hole.

He saw them drink and scamper away, rejoicing in their speed, challenging the horse-hunters to do their worst. And behind them, on his thorough-bred, the fat and burly Bodie, laying the rope across Fly's rump in sheer chagrin. He was a rough man, a hard man, and he had those in his gang who would not hesitate to kill if they could. But he was only a man, and the golden horses of Night Water belonged to the first one who came. They were wild horses, free to roam over the lim-itless sink, free to drink at twenty hidden springs; and the first man who could ride up on them and snare one with his rope could hold him against the world.

"Jack," announced Horse-Ketchum, as he watched the half-moon rise, "I want to go back—ketchum horse."

"Huh!" grunted the Indian, "Val Bodie—she kill you. How much you give me, I go?"

"How much you want?" countered Johnny, eagerly. But Captain Jack would not say.

"You afraid?" demanded Horse-Ketchum at last.

"No! No 'fraid nothing!" answered Jack valiantly. "You give me fi-ive hundred dollars—me go."

"Five hundred!" cried Lightfoot, not to yield too quick. "That's a whole lot of money, Jack. Don't you know it's against the law for an Injun to get rich? What the hell do you want with all that?"

"Buyum wife!" responded Captain Jack promptly, But Horse-Ketchum shook his head.

"Ump-umm!" he protested, "we've got troubles enough, already. Who'll help me ketch horses if you buy you a wife? All the time, you stay at home."

"Nope—five hundred dollars!" repeated the Indian expectantly, and Horse-Ketchum slapped him on the back.

"Say, who is this lady?" he bantered. "Another girl of Eatum-up Jake's?"

"No! *Good* woman!" stated Jack. "Maybeso Piute girl. You give me five hundred—me go."

"And you don't give a damn whether Bodie gets you or not, eh? All right, Jack—come on. It's a go!"

Captain Jack turned his horse and headed north by the stars and three nights later they rode into Night Water, where a horse-trap had been built, and torn down. Only the solid posts remained, set deep around the trench where the mustangs went down to drink. Horse-Ketchum and his Indian dismounted in the moonlight and sought long for human footprints. Val Bodie had built the fence and swung the huge gate—but who had torn it down?

"*No wano!*" pronounced Captain Jack, slapping his leg emphatically. And instinctively he raised his eyes to where, black and menacing, Devil Mountain towered above them like a wall. "No good!" he said again. "Yeller horse all go 'way. Maybeso devil-man come here!"

"Maybeso," agreed Horse-Ketchum. "Where you think horses go? You don't reckon Val Bodie caught 'em?"

"Nope! No ketchum!" decided Jack. "'Nother spring—over here." And he pointed towards the west.

They filed out across the flats, where the self-rising ground had puffed up and formed a hard crust; until at last a broader trail led them in to a hidden hole, where the burros had pawed out fresh dirt.

"Yeller horse!" exclaimed the Indian, pointing eagerly to a track; and once more Johnny saw the round, dainty hoof-marks, newly made in the trampled earth. But this water-hole lay in the open, amid hummocks of coarse grass, and surrounded by miles of the treacherous self-rising ground, where in a chase the best of horses might fall.

"We'll shirt-tail it!" he decided. And, hanging rags on stakes and strings, they went back to Night Water, to lie in wait when the wild horses came in.

For the same fear which had driven them to abandon their old watering-place would now send them back to Toógahboth. A rag fluttering in the wind, the suspicious line of white string, carelessly stretched to surround the water-hole, would conjure up visions of horse-hunters in hiding—and the fence around Night Water was old.

Many times, since it had been set and then torn down to the bare stakes, the golden horses must have circled it while the stallion snorted and whistled and the lead mare snuffed from afar. But now, driven by thirst, they would come back more eagerly. Horse-Ketchum left the water-hole undisturbed. All that day, making no smoke, they lay hid among the mesquite trees, where their animals could browse and eat beans. But though he waited for two nights, while the moon approached its full, only burros returned to the spring.

Captain Jack, torn with fear of the Indian devil of Enúpi Gai—whom he considered the protector of the horses—and yet resolute to win his five hundred dollars, lay hid day and night on the summit of a huge hummock, where the sand had buried a mesquite tree to its tips. Crouched down behind the brush he watched the cliffs with staring eyes, turning his head again and again to search the desert to the south for signs of Val Bodie and his band. There was danger on every side, but Horse-Ketchum would not give up. And that night the moon would be full.

"What's the matter, Jack?" he asked as they saddled up at sundown. "Don't you know some other place where maybe these horses drink? You think, now—some other spring!"

"Maybeso Hole-in-Rock," responded Captain Jack at last. "Me go up there tonight—puttum rock over hole. Then horse come down here—you ketchum."

"W'y, sure!" agreed Johnny. "Why the hell didn't you say so, instead of waiting around for three days?"

"Me no likum Hole-in-Rock," explained Jack. "Val Bodie ketch me there—she kill me."

"I see," nodded Lightfoot. "Well, don't let him ketch you, then. But you run those horses down here, where I can get one more chance at them, and I'll give you your money. You can go."

"You gimme five hundred dollars?" demanded Captain Jack eagerly. And Horse-Ketchum nodded grimly.

"You bet ye," he assented. "But you find them horses—savvy? This is getting kinder spooky, and first thing we know Val Bodie is liable to drop in on us. Have you seen that old devil-man today?"

"Me seeum!" stated the Indian, briefly. "You look out. Maybeso she kill you."

"Ye-es, she'll play hell—killing me!" scoffed Johnny. "I'll just plug Mister Injun devil, right where his suspenders cross, if he tries any rough work with me."

"You look out!" warned Captain Jack, swinging up into his saddle. "Tonight full moon—Injun devil makum medicine. Maybeso Val Bodie makum, too."

"I'll make a little, myself, then," promised Horse-Ketchum. And he slapped the worn holster of his gun.

As the sun sank in the west a great light appeared; as if, behind the mountains to the east, the world itself was afire. The sky was lit up with a red and yellow glow; until at last over Devil Mountain, like a ball of enameled gold, the moon rose up, majestically. Every crater on its surface seemed to stand out like a pit-hole, its huge ranges cast broad shadows across the plains; and the sun, scarcely hidden behind the rim of the world, made its sister of the night gleam like day.

Horse-Ketchum cinched up High Behind and took his post behind a tree; but his eyes, which at first were wary and intent, soon grew big with the wonder of the scene. Devil Mountain rose before him, its canyons deep and black, its high cliffs etched with lines of silvery light. And on the playa of the dry lake mystic figures appeared as the wild burros paced in towards the spring. In the moonlight their runty bodies were transformed to ghostly horses, their huge ears to crested manes; and, running dimly among them, he seemed to see silvery foxes that leapt up to kiss their noses as they passed.

It was the old moon madness coming back. But when the burros stumped past him to gather about the water-hole he laughed and shook out his rope. Let Jack see Indian devils, and maidens who rode by night on the backs of golden steeds—all he believed was what he saw, and not half of that. But this time there would be no delays. When the golden horses came he would ride out and make his throw. He would tie to the phantom stallion and let his rope be the judge—if it passed through him, then all was a dream.

Scuffling and braying in clownish abandon the burros drifted off, to graze on the coarse sacaton; and, keeping his long vigil, Horse-Ketchum dozed. He was fetched up standing by a shrill neigh from High Behind, a neigh that rose, eager and piercing, and ended in a snort as Johnny laid a hand on his nose. All was silent then and the broad, white lake-bed brought back no answer to his call; but in a tremble of excitement Lightfoot tightened his cinch and whipped the kinks out of his rope. Then he listened, and at last down the wind there came a whistle that he knew. The golden stallion had returned.

Across the playa something moved, something that seemed to glide on air; but Horse-Ketchum knew it was a band of wild horses, circling about before they came in to drink. They were tired, for they travelled at a walk. Weary miles lay behind them if they came from the spring where Jack had covered the hole with a stone. They were thirsty, and they broke into a trot.

Down the wind from the water-hole, behind a barricade of sand drifted up against the body of a tree, Horse-Ketchum stood watching in the blackest shade, twisting the hackamore on High Behind's nose. Man and horse were trembling now in anticipation of the chase, but Lightfoot's nerves were calm. He felt none of the indecision which had come over him before and held him back from the start—and yet he bided his time.

Weary and gaunted though they were the golden horses could still outrun him. He waited until the mare, stepping forward out of the band, went down into the trench to drink. Then he mounted silently, though the stallion snuffed the wind, holding back while his *manada* went in.

With heavy sighs, one by one, they backed out of the trench and stood drooping, while the others went down—yet Horse-Ketchum withheld his hand. The golden stallion still stood guard, shying suspiciously at the circle of posts which had been set when Bodie made his trap. And of all these glorious horses he was the noblest by far. Horse-Ketchum waited—for him.

Snuffing the wind, snuffing the sand with its faint human taint, his head pivoting as he scanned the shadowy trees, he entered at last into the circle of deepset stakes and glided down the incline to drink. Horse-Ketchum shook his rope out, his lips murmuring a sort of prayer as the last slow seconds passed. He felt exalted, almost religious, raised above his common self by the thought of what lay before him. One careful, measured rush—a flip of the rope—and the golden stallion was his! The most beautiful horse in the world.

He rode out slowly, hanging low behind his horse, and for a moment the mustangs were deceived. They stood staring, their heads erect, their nostrils quivering in frightened snorts, and Horse-Ketchum threw in the spurs. But though High Behind leapt forward in a series of mighty strides the wild horses galloped away—beyond the sweep of the rope, spurning the earth in a drumming stampede. Only the stallion, head down in the narrow trench, was left behind in the flight.

At the sudden rush of feet he backed out with a whistling snort. His wind-swept mane seemed to bristle as he faced the charging horseman. Then he whirled and dodged out between the posts of the half-wrecked trap, every muscle in furious action. The ground trembled beneath the impact of his racing feet, but High Behind was upon him, charging down in full stride, and Horse-Ketchum shook out his loop.

The reata whistled in swift circles as he poised for the throw. Then as the stallion straightened out into his swift, resistless pace Horse-Ketchum shot out his rope. They were running like the wind but the plaited rawhide went straight and true. The long loop hovered and spread, and settled around his neck. The golden stallion was snared. Horse-Ketchum took his dally and set High Behind up, leaning back to hold his saddle against the jerk. Then the stallion hit the rope and went tumbling, heels over head, and Horse-Ketchum took up his slack.

CHAPTER IX

A PRESENT FOR BODIE

LIKE a man who feels the tug of an enormous, fighting trout, which he had angled for long in some pool, and sets back, playing him warily; so Horse-Ketchum, the mustanger, thrilled all over at the jerk and gave the golden stallion more rope. But he did not run against the slack, to hurl himself once more, thrown and sprawling across the smooth sands. Somewhere before he had felt the bite of rope and he came at his captor, charging.

Horse-Ketchum threw off his turns and reined quickly aside, holding his coiled rope high for a flip. Then as the stallion wheeled and reared, his forefeet raised to strike, a loop came spinning down the rope. It encircled the poised feet like the writhing of a snake and the stallion fell heavily to the ground. Another loop followed, drawing the forefeet close together, and Horse-Ketchum stepped down from his horse.

In his hand he held a *jáquima*, the rawhide hack-amore of the horse-breaker—a heavy nose-piece of plaited thongs, rigged with ropes to form a halter which when pulled would cut off the breath. Waving his hat at High Behind to make him keep the reata taut, Johnny went down the rope to where the stallion had fallen and jumped spraddling on his neck. Over his nose with a practiced jerk he slipped the breaking-halter and adjusted it behind his ears. Then, with two ropes instead of one, he swung up on his mount and flipped off the binding loops.

The stallion came up snorting and Horse-Ketchum leaned back to meet the shock of another jerk. But somewhere this wild horse had learned the lesson of the rope, for now he did not run. He shook his head and looked around, every muscle a-tremble; then, facing the east, he neighed, long and shrill. But his *manada* did not respond. They had fled into the night—he was alone.

Horse-Ketchum rose up closer, pulling gently on his hackamore, and suddenly the wild mustang was tame. He yielded to the tug before the cruel *bosal* closed down against his sensitive nose, and when Johnny reined away he followed after him obediently, yet always with his eyes to the east. Again and again, like a quavering cry for help, he let out his piercing neigh; until at last, from the night, there came a distant answer, clear and high—the call of his mate.

Lightfoot leaned back and watched him, taking in with a lover's eyes every line of his beautiful prize—the small, sensitive ears, the full eyes, the flaring nostrils, the proud set to his head as he neighed. Every part of him seemed perfect, for endurance or speed—the straight back, the slender legs, the heavy muscles of shoulder and hip. He had all the points of a thoroughbred, and yet Death Valley was his home. Johnny spoke to him, softly, but now the stallion had turned and was gazing away to the south.

High Behind switched his ears and listened intently, his sensitive nose testing out the wind. Then he, too, gave a neigh; and soon across the lake Captain Jack rode up to them, laughing.

"Ketchum horse, hey?" he cried as he paused to survey the prize. "Me findum track at spring—put big rock on hole. Bimeby horse come—me driveum."

"Well, bully for you, Jack!" exclaimed Horse-Ketchum exultantly. And, whipping forth his pocketbook, he counted out five hundred dollars into the Indian's expectant hands.

"Now!" he went on, "let's get out of this country. Listen to that!" And the stallion neighed again.

"*No wano!*" warned Captain Jack. "You pullum rope—makeum stop. Injun devil, she come here, sure."

"Val Bodie's the only devil that I'm afraid of," answered Lightfoot. "What's the quickest way out—straight north?"

76

"Go Hole-in-Rock," responded Jack. "Ketchum water—hide all day. This horse, she fight like hell."

"No. No fight!" declared Johnny. "Look here, how he leads." And he started slowly off across the lake.

"Too good—that horse," observed Captain Jack cynically. "You look out—maybeso she kill you."

"Kill—nothing!" retorted Horse-Ketchum. "He's gentle, I tell you. Somebody else has caught him, before."

"Maybeso somebody else ketch us," grumbled the Indian. And he loped off to pack up the mules.

They pulled out on the run, the golden stallion following free as they rode away across the dry lake; but when they turned into the trail that led east to Hole-in-the-Rock he set back and fought the rope.

"Yeah—she tame!" jeered Captain Jack riding warily in behind him. And as Horse-Ketchum reined his mount to keep clear of the thrashing slack he laid his quirt across the stallion's rump. He jumped forward, striving purposely to entangle his captor. Then with teeth bare and gleaming he charged back at the Indian, who promptly took to the brush.

"Leave him alone!" ordered Horse-Ketchum, after the flurry was over. And, setting back gently on the hackamore, he cut off the stallion's breath. Three times he pulled and slackened, and then with a great sigh the golden horse accepted his fate. At the tug of the rope he followed along obediently, but at every turn and corner he looked back. Up the smooth, hard stream-bed, laid down by some cloudburst, they swung along at a rapid trot—past the Breyfogle Buttes, past the looming point of rocks and into the dark canyon beyond. Hole-in-the-Rock lay before them, with its dim trail up to the spring; when suddenly, out of the darkness, they rode forth into bright moonlight, and with a snort the stallion began to buck. Out of the corner of his eye Horse-Ketchum saw the pack-mules, fleeing madly back down the gulch. He glimpsed Jack, whipping after them—and other forms that meant nothing as he clung to the saddle and rope.

High Behind was jumping in circles to keep the slack from under his heels, Johnny was playing the bounding stallion like a fish; when from the blur of movement about him a rawhide rope came *slap,* and his arms were pinned to his sides. Another loop roped the stallion—they came pelting in like rain, and he found himself jerked to the ground. Then as his head ceased to spin he saw horsemen all about him, and Val Bodie looking down at him, laughing.

"I got ye, eh?" he taunted, swinging down from his horse and snatching Johnny's gun from its holster. "Red-handed, by grab, but I'll have to admit it—you're the most accommodating and obliging son-of-a-goat that I've met with in many a day. You not only ketch my horse but you bringing him right to me!" And he leaned back, shaking with laughter.

"And he got the stud, too!" shouted Hank Boots triumphantly, "the best danged horse in the band. If that ain't being clever, what is?"

"One good turn deserves another," chuckled Bodie. "Just for that, boys, we'll let him live. Turn him loose, to rustle. Maybe next time we ketch him he'll have us another fine horse."

He glanced across admiringly at the stallion and as Horse-Ketchum felt the sting of their laughter he fought against the ropes, cursing furiously. After all his hard riding, his weeks of danger and toil, he had ridden into the hands of his enemy. But he would not give up the horse.

"You leave him alone!" he shouted. "I caught him, and by the gods, he's mine. You steal that horse and I'll come and steal him back. He's mine, I say—he's mine!"

"That'll do, now," warned Bodie, jabbing a gun against his ribs. "It's no trouble at all to throw a rope around your neck and drag you to death over the rocks. That's what I intended to do when I rode down to the spring and found where you'd covered up the water. That's a crime, out on this desert—the worst crime of all. But nobody can say that Val Bodie ain't generous; and young man, you've sure done me a good turn. With this stud here for bait I can build me another trap and ketch every mare in that band.

"Now think this matter over and don't speak too hastily—don't say anything that you're liable to regret. Didn't I understand you to say you was bringing me back this horse; being as I told you, once before, he was mine?"

He put up his pistol and dropped a loop over Lightfoot's head, and Horse-Ketchum saw he was whipped.

"Well—take him," he answered sullenly.

"I'll do that," responded Bodie, "and thankee kindly, stranger. You're not such a fool as I thought. I was going to strip you clean and turn you loose on the desert with your hands tied behind you, barefoot. Now there's another little thing that I'd kinder like to have—as a memento, you might say, of our meeting. Something to remind me of you, when you're gone. You mentioned one time a piece of rock you had. I'd like that Breyfogle ore."

"What is this?" demanded Johnny, "a hold-up? Are you going to steal everything I've got?"

"No, not if you're reasonable," answered Bodie. "All I want is that piece of rock."

"And if I give it to you," bargained Lightfoot, "will you let me have my horse, to get out of this cursed country?"

"You can have Old Hump-back," replied Bodie, scornfully. "Only be damned sure you keep a-going. Don't let me ketch you back again, mixing up in my affairs and trying to find my mine. Because if I do I'll beef you, for a certainty."

"Take these ropes off," ordered Horse-Ketchum fretfully. And when his hands were freed he fetched out the precious specimen and handed it over to Bodie.

"Well and good," observed the saloon-keeper, looking it over by moonlight and thrusting it into his pocket. "Now I'll just take your gun and pistol, so there won't be no argument about it. And yonder, up the canyon, is your road."

He flipped off the last reata and Horse-Ketchum took the road. But at the turn of the canyon he stopped. He was unarmed, but he was free; and somewhere in the hills Captain Jack would be watching for his smoke. Val Bodie had twenty men and they were only two, but Horse-Ketchum had gazed upon the beauty of the moon horses and he reined back into the Valley of Death.

CHAPTER X

THE HORSE-TRAP

ON the south flank of Breyfogle Butte, as the moon sank low, a fire flared up and died down suddenly, then leapt up with a fiercer glow. It winked out and blazed forth again for as long as a desert greasewood could give off its feeble flame; and at last, far down on the floor of Death Valley, an answering signal shot up. Two fires, side by side, and Horse-Ketchum knew that his faithful Indian had seen.

An hour later they came together in a rocky wash, Captain Jack hanging back and sending his pack animals ahead, for fear of another trap. He stepped out of a black shadow when he heard his master's voice; but his old confidence was gone and he hung his head in silence, as if expecting a just rebuke. For at the first sign of danger he had whirled and fled as if the devil of the mountain was after him.

"Well, Jack," spoke up Horse-Ketchum, "I reckon here's where we part. Val Bodie took my horse and I'm going back after him. All I want is some grub—and your gun."

"My gun!" repeated the Indian. "What for?"

"Never mind," answered Lightfoot. "Val Bodie took mine—and this one is no good to you, nohow. You take the outfit and wait for me at Pahrump. Hurry up and open up that pack!"

He stuffed a flour-sack with jerked meat and a little bread and coffee, then fished out his spare pistol from the bottom of a kyack and strapped it around his waist.

"Where you go now?" demanded Captain Jack. gruffly. "Maybeso Val Bodie kill you."

"Well, he'll never get you," rejoined Johnny sarcastically. "So come ahead—gimme that gun. All you need is a pair of spurs when it comes to a fight. You're brave as hell—ain't you, Jack?"

"What for me git killed?" defended Captain Jack indignantly. "Me seeum plenty men—all ride up at once. Me see horse buck—no can leadum away."

"Nope—I lost him," agreed Lightfoot. "But the show ain't over yet. Only I can't whip twenty men with one old six-shooter. So what about that one of yours?"

Captain Jack fingered ruefully the butt of his precious pistol, the symbol of his warrior's estate. But he had not made good on his oft-repeated boasts, and at last he unbuckled his belt.

"You takum," he said. "Me wait for you—Pahrump. Maybeso me no see you again."

"Don't you worry," responded Horse-Ketchum grimly. "You've got five hundred dollars and all the time in the world. Now you stay there, savvy, until I come."

"All right," agreed Captain Jack and turned the mules back into the hills, to make a dry camp for the day.

Horse-Ketchum rode back north, straight for the Breyfogle Buttes, and at daylight he crept out on a point and trained his glasses on Night Water. There were men there, cutting mesquite poles and setting posts around the spring, where their water-trap had been destroyed. And, tied to a heavy stake for his mates to see, the golden stallion stood drooping. Johnny muttered to himself and scanned the desert floor, where in great reaches of gravel and broad, alkali-whitened flats Lost Valley stretched away into the haze. Here and there on the wide expanse he spied burros in twos and threes, grazing on salt-grass or browsing on mesquite-tips; but nowhere within the sweep of his field-glasses could he pick up the golden herd.

They had fled to some canyon in the distant mountains or quit the country for good; but all through the day Val Bodie's men worked on, until their horse-pen and trap were complete. Then as evening approached they mounted and rode away, leaving the stallion to fret at his stake. Nothing stirred in the thicket of trees that lined the edge of the dry lake, and the horsemen rode back the way they came; but Horse-Ketchum had counted them—and he knew Bodie's horse. There were six men hiding by the trap.

Night came and he crept back to where High Behind was hid and rode down to an alkali spring, but as the moon came up he moved in towards his magnet—the horse he had won, and lost. So brief had been the time of his joyous possession, so urgent the necessity to escape, that he had never laid a hand on that glorious head and neck, except to fasten a rope. Fighting his head and pulling back the golden stallion had done his best to escape his inevitable fate. And then, while the battle for supremacy still raged, Val Bodie had captured them both.

Not once had Horse-Ketchum stroked his vel-vety nose or brushed back the flowing mane. It was a fight, from the start, but even while they struggled his heart had gone out to his prize. He fought with a courage that knew no defeat; yielding only to bide his time for another, more reckless break to gain the freedom he loved. Yet now he stood, anchored fast to a stake, to serve as a lure for his mates.

From the far end of the dry lake Lightfoot edged in towards him, keeping back under cover of the brush. He had circled Night Water, to come in against the wind, which was blowing up strong from the south. The air was full of sand and out across the playa dead sticks and wisps of grass went flying past. It was a good night for a task as desperate as his, for every limb and bush was on the move. Even the moon was half obscured by the smudge of rolling dust—he crept up till he saw the stallion.

A massive snubbing-post had been set before the spring; and, half hidden by brush, two wings had been constructed, leading into a pen behind. Then the builders had ridden away, leaving the stallion for a lure. And somewhere among the trees lurked the mustangers. Horse-Ketchum came on warily, his eyes on the thrashing branches that masked every movement behind. At any moment from that thicket Val Bodie might charge out at him, and then the best he could hope for was a running fight, with High Behind out in front.

He was a horse that had no equal among the

mounts of the Night Riders. Not even Bodie's Fly could keep up with him on the level, and across the rocky draws he was invincible. In no more time than it took to leap up on his back Johnny would be safe from his enemies' pursuit. And if they came on shooting he would stand and shoot back, for nothing was gained by flight.

Horse-Ketchum had come to steal back his horse, and all the long night lay before him. He took shelter behind a mesquite tree and watched. All day Bodie's riders had toiled hard, building the trap. The night before they had been in the saddle. What would be more natural, if no wild horses came, than for the hunters to fall asleep? Lightfoot kept on his feet, to fight off the sleep that came over him, and the moon swung up to its zenith.

The wind went down, leaving the air still and murky, and the stallion began to fight at his stake. He set back against the rope, trying the hackamore with all his strength; but it held and he quit with a grunt. His proud head drooped again and he stood patiently waiting the next move in a losing game. Wild burros came trooping in, to snort their distrust as they gazed at the fenced-in hole, and suddenly the golden stallion pricked his ears to the east. He neighed, and there came an answering call.

The burros stood staring, Horse-Ketchum tightened his cinch, and across the silvery lake-bed a single horse trotted in—it was the lead mare, returning to her mate. Now the chance had come for which Lightfoot had waited. There would be mounting and riding, a chase across the playa— and while Bodie and his riders sought to pen the faithful mare the stallion would be left unguarded. He backed deeper into the thicket, while out across the lake the mare came trotting, head up.

Johnny gazed at her covetously as, half revealed by the dim moonlight, she circled and snuffed the wind. She wheeled and raced away, but soon she was back again, whickering softly to her captive mate. She advanced and set her feet, ready to whirl and run at the first sign of impending pursuit. But she came on, almost to him, and something in her gait suddenly caught Horse-Ketchum's trained eye. She traveled like a horse that was rode.

She whirled as if to flee, and above her floating mane Johnny saw a head bob up. It was the head of the moon-maiden, lying close to the golden mane which mingled with her own flowing hair; and as the mare wheeled, snorting, he saw the form of the rider, clinging close to her side like a bat. With a quick slap at her head she brought her mount up to the stake. Then suddenly she leaned down and cut the stallion's rope loose, and Horse-Ketchum knew she was a woman.

Living with Indians so much and listening to their talk he had come almost to believe in their stories of devils and ghosts. Almost, and not to oppose him, he had conceded to Captain Jack the presence of a devil on Enúpi Gai—a man-devil who watched over the ghost-horses. But, when his rope had snared its neck, the ghost-stallion had proved real—and now the ghost-maiden had flashed a knife.

She rose up triumphantly as the tie-rope was slashed and headed the stallion back towards the hills. But as he jumped to escape, his forefeet were jerked from under him and he fell sprawling—he was hobbled, to boot. Then a yell went up from a thin fringe of mesquite trees that extended out into the lake, and six riders came dashing forth. Their ropes were swinging, they leaned forward against the wind, and their horses came on at a gallop.

The moon-maiden turned to flee, then she dropped to the ground and ran back to the struggling horse. Like a flash the startled mare made a break to escape, but a rope brought her up with a jerk. The woman was stooping over to cut the stallion loose when a reata dropped over her head. Six riders with six ropes made their casts into the scramble, and every loop fell true.

"Well, my Gawd!" whooped Bodie as he set up his horse, "look what I got, while the getting was good! A girl, and a damned pretty girl!"

He dropped down and grabbed her as she threw off the rope. There was a struggle and a woman's piercing scream. Then Horse-Ketchum, forgetting his mission, charged down on them, cursing. Val Bodie had the girl in his arms.

CHAPTER XI

THE MOON-MAIDEN

A FIERY rage had swept over Horse-Ketchum at the first shriek of the moon-maiden, whom Bodie had roped as she fought. Johnny had come there to win back his horse but he cast the thought aside and rode in on them, shooting furiously. The horse-hunters stampeded as if blown by a wind, carried away by the panic of their mounts, and as Bodie saw the flash of a gun in his face he ran without firing a shot. Lightfoot hurled one pistol after him and swung down by the struggling stallion, throwing the girl the rope of her mare.

"There's your horse—now ride!" he panted; and stooped down to cut loose the tangled stallion. He leapt in on him recklessly, feeling about for the rawhide hobbles, straightening up to get out his knife. Then, sitting on his neck, he slashed the hobbles loose and the stallion came to his feet. But as he plunged out into the night Horse-Ketchum grabbed the hackamore and sat back on the rope. They fought each other desperately, each intent on his own escape; but man, the master, won and Johnny swung up on High Behind with the halter-rope wrapped around the horn.

For one instant, exultantly, he glanced back at the mesquite thicket where Bodie and his riders had fled. Then he turned towards the north, leaning forward against the tug as the stallion resisted the rope. Johnny's chance had come, and he had seized it. Now the stallion was his, and the woman was already forgotten. He had scattered the mustangers and won back his prize, the glorious golden stallion of his dreams. He sunk the spurs into High Behind at sight of a man running towards him, but as his mount plunged forward a shotgun blazed and he felt the burn of shot across his back. The gun belched again and High Behind fell to bucking—bucking and running and squealing with pain.

Horse-Ketchum grabbed the horn, turning sideways to dodge the rope which was towing the stallion behind, and they took off across the dry lake. High Behind's tail was clenched down, his rump was twisted sidewise as he shrank from the hurt of the shots; but angrily, bawling and lashing, he bucked out into the night while Horse-Ketchum rode him, reeling. The grip of his knees had weakened, his hand was wet as he grasped the rope; but through the storm of whirling and bucking he kept his turns on the horn. The golden stallion was his!

They went galloping, across the lake-bed and out into the rocks where a great sand-wash came down from the hills, and here Horse-Ketchum suddenly learned why the stallion had led so free. He was following after his mate, the mare. She had come down from Devil Mountain to seek him when he was caught, and now he was heading towards home. But High Behind, shrinking and side-winding from the burn of the buckshot, climbed the cut-bank and headed north; and as they started to leave the wash the golden stallion set back, jerking the saddle until it slipped.

For an instant Horse-Ketchum clung desperately with his spurs, while High Behind leaped and writhed. Then the latigo popped and he went backwards through the air, still clinging to the stallion's rope. He felt the scratch of thorny bushes, the impact of polished stones. He gripped the hackamore, and his light went out.

When he came out of his trance he was riding again, only now he was tied to the horn. And the horse that he rode was not rough old High Behind but the golden stallion of his dreams. They were trotting up a canyon so deep and narrow that the walls cut out the light of the moon; but before him, leading the way, Johnny could see another horseman. Then he went out again, and woke up groaning.

He lay face-down across the saddle, lashed on like a deer, and on his lips there was the salt taste of blood. Ropes bit at his wrists and ankles, his back burned like fire and his head seemed encased in an iron band, against which his pulse-beat throbbed furiously. His brain reeled and he was conscious only of the gentle motion of his steed, an ambling trot that lulled him to sleep.

He woke again, long after, and he was lying in a cave from whose roof, like crystal pendants, long stalactites hung down, with an eerie suggestion of splendor. In the pale light of dawn bats were fluttering past his couch, seeking their clinging-places in the darkness beyond. Horse-Ketchum sat up, laying one hand on his throbbing head, and at a stab of pain he clutched at his back. His shirt was wet with blood.

For an instant, seeing the splendor of the crystals overhead and the eerie bats flitting past, he had wondered whether he was in heaven or hell. But at the feel of the fresh blood it came back to him instantly—the fight over the horses, the sting of buckshot as he fled, then the ride up a dark, narrow canyon. But who had brought him up there? And why had they left him, to welter uncared for in his blood? He listened intently as a distant noise came to his ears—then clear and distinct, he heard the *whang* of a heavy rifle and a staccato of answering shots. A battle was on, and at the memory of Val Bodie he rolled over and crept out of the cave.

A tangle of wild clematis hung down over its entrance and as he peered out he saw the stallion over which they had fought, standing tied and still burdened with his saddle. There was a fence across the canyon, ancient willows lined the creek, and over the white stones a stream of water flowed, crystal clear, inviting him to drink. He rose weakly to his feet and staggered down to its brink, and as he drank and washed his face the stallion nickered appealingly, pulling back against his rope.

"Poor old horse," murmured Johnny, crawling over to the tree. And with the last of his strength he untied the tangled ropes and let him go down to the creek. Then he dropped back exhausted, for every effort he made started his wounds to bleeding afresh. The stallion sighed and sipped again, but at a noise from down the canyon he snorted and raised his head. Horse-Ketchum heard the sound of approaching feet and wriggled feebly back towards the cave, but half-way across the open the last of his strength left him and he fell face-down in the dirt.

Someone came and stood over him. He saw the tip of a buckskin moccasin and the butt of a gun on the ground. But as he raised his eyes he beheld a woman's face, surrounded by a nimbus of golden hair. It was the moon-maiden, flushed and hurried, and even as she gazed she turned and looked behind her.

"Who are you?" she asked in a low, anxious voice. "I found you last night and hid you in the cave. If my father finds you here he will kill you."

"Name's Lightfoot," responded Johnny. "I saw you—down at Night Water. But somebody shot me in the back."

"That was Val Bodie," she said. "He tried to steal Paynim, and now he's coming up the canyon. Let me drag you into the cave, where nobody will find you. Because I can't bear to see you killed."

"Neither can I," grumbled Horse-Ketchum grimly. "Can't you do something for my back?"

"Not now," she answered, taking hold of his hands and dragging him, willy-nilly, into the cave. "My father sent me back to get some more cartridges." And, dropping him inside the entrance, she deftly wiped out his tracks and sped away down the trail.

Horse-Ketchum thrust out his head and stared after her curiously, as she darted into another and larger cave. Its door was only a cowhide, suspended by strips of rawhide; but when she came out she bore an armful of cartridge-boxes, which she dropped into her buckskin skirt. Then, snatching up her rifle, she ran off down the trail as swift and agile as a deer.

"My Lord!" he breathed, as the shooting burst out afresh, "she's a fighter, or I miss my guess. But how in the hell did *she* get up this canyon? And that horse I stole is *tame!*"

He glanced across the creek, where the golden stallion was peacefully feeding, and his eyes grew big as he watched. Here was the leader of the wild horses that he had chased at Night Water, and that Val Bodie had tried so long to trap, browsing placidly on willow shoots not ten feet away from him—with a saddle on his back! It was Horse-Ketchum's own saddle, and the hackamore on its nose was the one he had put there himself. Yet down on the dry lake-bed the stallion had fought like the devil—like the wildest of untamed mustangs.

"Here, Paynim!" he called softly, using the name he had heard her use; and the horse pricked his ears and stared. But Paynim remembered the battles they had fought—he snorted and drew away. "A regular pet," muttered Johnny, looking him over enviously. And then, at a thought, he glanced up and down the canyon for some possible way of escape. But it was boxed in—there was no way out. He was trapped within these walls that rose thousands of feet high, and only the good will of this woman could save him, for he was wounded and unable to ride. Yet he was the man who had stolen Paynim, and Bodie had only taken the horse from him.

There was a boom from down the canyon, the loud-mouthed roar of a rifle, and a crackling of distant shots. Bodie had discovered at last the hidden pasture of the horses and he was trying to force his way in. If he succeeded, then Horse-Ketchum could look for no mercy, for he had robbed Val Bodie of his prey. Next to whisky he loved women—and the golden horses of Toógahboth had long been the apple of his eye. Yet Lightfoot at one stroke had deprived him of both prizes—the moon-maiden and the stallion she rode.

Horse-Ketchum listened anxiously as the shooting came nearer. Yet even if Bodie failed to force the narrow passageway, what hope had the future for him? The girl herself had told him that her father would kill him if he found him in his hidden retreat. He crawled back from the entrance to the shelter of some pack-saddles, and crouched down to endure his pain; until at last, outlined against the light of the entrance, he saw a head bob up. It dodged back, and for a moment he felt the cold fear of death. Then it rose up again and his blurred eyes caught the vision of a nimbus of golden hair. The maiden had come back, but she was looking behind her down the canyon, and he heard the sullen roar of guns.

She stood at gaze, like a sentinel guarding the secret of the cave. Then she stooped down suddenly and crept in towards him, and he felt her hot breath on his cheek. She leaned closer, feeling his face with small, clutching hands as if she feared to find him dead, and a quick tear splashed down between.

"He is coming," she gasped. "You must stay here and hide." And she dropped a bundle of food and fled. But of this man who came Horse-Ketchum knew nothing, except that his coming meant death.

CHAPTER XII

FROM KENTUCKY

THE noise of gunfire ceased abruptly and Horse-Ketchum lay listening for the sound of approaching footsteps—for the big, booming voice of his enemy, Val Bodie, or the voice of the moon-maiden's father. Whoever he was he had inspired in his daughter a fear fully as great as that of the ruthless Bodie, who had promised to shoot Lightfoot on sight. But no footsteps came and Horse-Ketchum became conscious of a hunger that gnawed at his vitals. Even while he listened for the coming of his enemies he ate ravenously of the dried meat and bread.

They had had a battle at the entrance to the canyon, that same narrow gateway between frowning walls of schist that Horse-Ketchum had watched through his glasses. It was not hard to guess who the Indian devil was who had terrorized the Indians for years. He was a white man, the owner of the band of golden horses which watered at Toógahboth spring. And when at last his stallion had been caught and the secret of his hiding-place discovered, the old man had cast aside all pretense of being a devil and stepped into the open, shooting.

Hours of waiting dragged by and a fox peered

into the cave, attracted by the smell of the meat. But when Horse-Ketchum stirred he scampered away, only to creep back, accompanied by his mate. They came closer, with that strange tameness which the wild stallion had shown, and Lightfoot remembered the silver foxes which had run at the horses' heads. The foxes, the horses, even the ghost-maiden that rode them when the moon was at its full, all were mortal as himself—all dwelt in this hidden canyon. And the Indian devil of Enúpi Gai was the master of them all. Johnny threw out scraps of meat for the foxes to gnaw on and dozed off into a fevered sleep.

He was awakened by a hand laid upon his brow, and the moon-maiden leaned over him, smiling. She had crept in unperceived and he caught the smell of arnica as he felt a wet cloth on his head.

"It is all right," she said soothingly. "The men have gone away and my father is guarding the gateway. Just let me bathe your head and put some medicine on your wounds—and when you are well you can go."

She washed the blood from the matted bruise, where he had fallen among the rocks, and Horse-Ketchum lay quiet as with a pan of hot water she soaked off his dirt-incrusted shirt.

"Oh!" she exclaimed as in the half light of the cave she beheld his quivering back. "Did he do that—the man who caught me?"

"I reckon so," shuddered Lightfoot. "Feel around

for those buckshot. Don't mind if I kick—dig 'em out."

"They went in and came out again," she said at last, after following the course of the shots. "You must have been leaning over when he shot."

"Mighty lucky," he grumbled. "Poor old High Behind got the most of it. Well, bandage me up good, so I can get out of here tonight. And put on lots of arnica."

"You'd better stay," she suggested as she worked over the wounds. "You'll die if you don't lie still. And if you go outside those bad men will kill you. Stay here—I'll keep you hid."

"What will your old man say if he finds me?" he demanded. And she blushed and turned away.

"I—I'll hide you," she promised. "Although he says that all men are bad. He says the first man that gets in here and gets out again alive will come back and take everything we've got."

"Oho!" spoke up Johnny. "So that's what's the matter with him! He's afraid of losing his horse."

"He says men are all bad, and we ought to keep away from them," she said with a fleeting smile. "But—but I've never seen any, so how can I tell? That is, until I saw you."

"Never seen any men?" repeated Horse-Ketchum incredulously. "Been shut up in this canyon all your life?"

"I've seen them riding by," she admitted. "But he drives every man away."

"He must be crazy," he muttered. "But say, I saw you once—down on the lake-bed."

"He doesn't know it," she confessed, "but I go down there at night. When the moon shines it seems as if these big walls would smother me. I've just got to get out and see the great world. And we turn out the horses then. At first there were only four of them, but now we have eleven and there isn't enough grass up the canyon. So every full moon Father opens the lower gate and lets them go down on the plain. Isn't it beautiful down there, at night?"

"It's like a dream," he answered. "The first time I saw you I thought you had come down from the moon."

"Oh, did you?" she cried, laughing rapturously. "Did you see me down there—riding? I get so lonely I just can't stand it—but what were *you* doing at Night Water?"

"I've heard about the horses, and how beautiful they were," he evaded. "So I went there and hid— to watch them."

"If Father had seen you," she began; then stopped and bit her lip. "He kills people," she said at last.

"So I've heard," he nodded. "But what does he do it for? I thought the horses were wild!"

"Oh, he's—strange," she replied, bandaging his wounds up nervously. "He's afraid they'll steal his mine."

"Mine!" he echoed, startled.

"He's got one—somewhere," she stated. But Johnny knew there was only one "somewhere" where the mine was likely to be hid, and that was right up that canyon. But she had already told him too much and he did not pursue the subject.

"Oh, that's nothing," he laughed. "All these old prospectors are that way. And they think it's worth millions and millions!"

"Yes—he does," she admitted naively. "All he thinks about is gold. He talks to himself, and threatens to kill people if they follow him back to his mine."

"You look out," warned Horse-Ketchum, "that he doesn't kill *you*. I believe your old man is crazy."

"He acts very strange," she said. "And Mother, before she died, told me to run away somewhere. But there isn't any place I can go. I never believed before that men were so cruel—he claims they're just like beasts. But when Val Bodie caught me— down at the lake last night—"

She bowed her head, to wink back the tears, and Johnny struggled up from where he lay.

"Now here," he began, "don't you worry about *him*. I'll take care of you, Pet. What's your name?"

"Diana," she sobbed, "Diana Morgan. But if Father finds you here I know he will kill you. And maybe he'll kill me, too."

She dropped her head against his breast and burst

out weeping and Horse-Ketchum held her help-lessly. Here was a woman so innocent she was no more than a child, and yet as he felt her warm body against his he experienced a strange sort of fear. She was a woman too innocent for the great world outside—too innocent to be lying in his arms. He was afraid, and yet he thrilled at her touch.

"Never mind, now," he soothed, "I'll try and come back for you if I ever get out of here alive. And if you'll give me a gun I'll protect you against your father, in case he tries to kill you. But you'd better go away, before he comes back and finds us. And besides, you don't know who I am."

"Yes, I do!" she answered, looking up with a smile as she brushed away a tear. "I was watching when you crawled out and untied Paynim, so he could go to the creek and drink."

"I like horses," admitted Johnny, "and that's why I done it. But your old man was right, and don't you forget it—most men are a mighty rough lot."

"But didn't you ride in, when Val Bodie caught me, and make him let me go? Oh, I'll never forget how terrible it was, when he grabbed me—and began to laugh!"

She shuddered and Horse-Ketchum let her lie where she was until her fit of weeping had passed. He even stroked her hair and told her not to cry. And then he tried again.

"Now, listen," he began, "and I'll tell you how that happened—and the kind of hombre I am. I didn't come down there to save you. I'm a horse-ketcher, savvy? And I came there to ketch that horse. I seen him tied to the stake and I was just sneaking up when you rode in, on that beautiful mare—and of course I had to hide. But when Bodie jumped out and grabbed you I'll have to admit I was mad. So I rode in on him shooting and gave you back your horse, while I cut loose the hobbles on Paynim. That's what I was there for—to get away with *him*. And if Bodie hadn't run out and filled me full of buckshot you'd never seen your Paynim-horse again."

"What? Were you trying to steal Paynim?" she demanded indignantly, suddenly bounding up to her feet. "Why, when I found you wounded, Paynim was standing right over you. He knew you had saved him and he wouldn't stir a step until I put you up on his back!"

"He's a wonderful horse!" sighed Johnny, "the most beautiful horse I've seen. That's why I wanted to steal him."

"Steal Paynim!" she cried. "Don't you know what would have happened to you? My father would have followed you and killed you, then and there! That's *his* way of dealing with horse-thieves!"

"I reckon so," responded Horse-Ketchum, stretching out on the bed to ease his aching back. "But say, Pet—or Diana, or whatever your name is—don't you think you'd better go? Because if your old man finds me, who'll come back and take care of you, when you try to leave this hole?"

"Well, it won't be any horse-thief!" she flared back angrily. "Because that's one thing that Father just hates. When Paynim was stolen he rode clear to Mormon Lake, on purpose to kill Val Bodie. But while he was gone Bodie's men came back, and I saw Paynim tied to that stake. If I had just waited a little longer, Father would have killed them all. And so you're a horse-thief, too?"

"Well, you might call it that, if you were mad enough," said Johnny. "I thought the horses were wild."

"What—those horses!" she laughed. "Can't you tell a real thoroughbred? Why, Selim, Paynim's father, was the best horse in Kentucky, when my father brought him west. They're race-horses! Of course they're not wild!"

"They didn't have any brands," defended Horse-Ketchum. "How the hell could I tell they were yours? Nobody knowed that you lived here—and they don't know yet. Go on, now, and leave me alone!"

She drew away from him hatefully, as if at her feet a rattlesnake had given his warning. Then she turned and started away, but at the mouth of the cave she came back.

"Here's some water," she said, throwing down a canteen. "And I'll bring you some grub, by-and-by. But I'll give you to understand I'm a Morgan from Kentucky, and no man can sass me like that."

"All right," mumbled Horse-Ketchum. But when she was gone he sat up and felt his bruised head. He had lost the power to think, to extricate himself from difficulties; and now he had offended the only person in the world who could get him out of that canyon alive. She was lonely, like a child shut up in a closet or a man lost on some desert island. He should have treated her gently, instead of sending her away and bragging about stealing her horse. But the gold mine, the thoroughbreds, the Morgans of Kentucky! He felt his head again and muttered to himself. Perhaps he had bumped it a little too hard.

CHAPTER XIII

FRYING-PAN'S MINE

HORSE-KETCHUM fell asleep with a feeling of guilt, of misfortune and of worse to come. He woke up sweating, a roaring voice in his ears—a man cursing as few men can curse. Crouching low he peered out, expecting to see him at the cave mouth; but the voice came from further away.

"Damn them all!" it thundered. "They are trying to steal my mine. They are trying to get my horses and dishonor my daughter. They are nothing but scoundrels and cut-throats. But I killed one—I saw him fall—and the rest slunk away—Val Bodie and his scurvy crew! By the gods, how I would love to stand them in a row and kill them, a man at a time!"

In the bright light outside Lightfoot could see the man pace by, a rifle in his hand, only his buckskin leggings showing as he strode up the trail to the fence.

"Hey, Selim!" he called, with senile joviality. "Hey, Turco—hey, Regulus—how are you? Did those rascally half-breeds try to trap you at the water-hole? And here's my noble Paynim, as I live! Diana, how did Paynim get back? Come up here—can't you hear me talking?"

Johnny saw her moccasins as she hurried past and then in a low voice she began to tell her story.

"What's that?" he bellowed. "You say Bodie had him caught and staked out in front of his trap? Now tell me the truth—who helped you get him back? I know you couldn't do it by yourself!"

"I don't know who he was," she answered meekly. "But a man on a high-backed horse who had been hiding among the trees rode out and cut the hobbles. He threw me Moonbeam's rope and told me to ride—"

"Moonbeam!" he broke in, "did they have her tied up, too?"

"Well—no," she faltered. "I rode down to get Paynim and the horse-hunters dashed out and caught her. They caught me, too, but this man charged in shooting and drove the whole band away. And then he gave me the ropes and told me to ride—and just as I looked back, Bodie shot him."

"Poor fellow!" pronounced her father. "Some member of the band in whom a spark of chivalry still lived. And so Bodie murdered him—but what was that about his horse? You say he was very high behind?"

"Yes, and straddled when he loped. I didn't see him distinctly—"

"Hah! I know the rascal well!" exclaimed her father, triumphantly. "He's a wolf in sheep's clothing if he pretended to turn Paynim loose. I saw him at Mormon Lake, where he raced Bodie's Fly and asked me to hold the stakes. He's a horse-hunter himself and he came in on purpose to catch our horses and sell them. He was traveling with an Injun, a cursed Shooshonnie that was always trying to track me to my mine. Until I laid for him one day and put a bullet through his neck. You say Val Bodie killed him?"

"They were fighting," she evaded, "and I saw his horse run past. But don't you think he was a very kind man?"

"He's a rascal, I tell you!" the old man thundered. "Every man in this country is a scoundrel and an outlaw. They've all fled here to escape punishment for their crimes. There isn't an honest man in all this broad country—they're all criminals and fugitives from justice, ready to prey on anyone they meet. And as for this gay young blade who saved you so handsomely, he's a mustanger by profession and enjoys the cognomen of Horse-Ketchum—bestowed by his Injun friend!"

"Why, I think," she defended, "that's a very pretty name. And I wished I could have thanked him for saving my life. He saved Paynim and Moonbeam, too."

"Yes! He saved them!" mocked her father. "But if Bodie had let him live you'd have seen this same Horse-Ketchum, riding off across the valley with both of them. I know him, for I heard him defy Bodie himself when he warned him out of the country. He had a specimen of the rock that Breyfogle found—the identical ore of my mine. Washed out, I suppose, by some terrific cloudburst and picked up as the Dutchman wandered past. But now that my hiding-place has been discovered by these rascals I'll play the last card I've got. I'm going back to drill some more holes under that gateway and blow the whole wall down."

"Oh, and shut us all in?" she cried. "Then how will we ever get out?"

"That is something," he said, "which gives me no concern whatever. Val Bodie has found me and he'll never give up till he forces his way up this canyon. But I'll show the scoundrelly rogue that a Morgan can not be intimidated. I'm a fighter—it's bred in the bone."

"But Father," she pleaded, "we'll run out of food. And besides, I don't want to be shut in!"

Her voice rose with tragic intensity but he answered her impatiently, and Horse-Ketchum heard him striding past. But now he knew who this devil-man was—he was Frying-pan George, the prospector. He it was who had shot Captain Jack in the neck. He had been at Mormon Lake when the horse-race had been run, and held the stakes—and the ore! What chance then for Johnny if the half-crazed old prospector found him hiding inside his canyon?

He lay listening to the sound of drills and hammers clinking together, while above the clatter of steel he could hear Diana's father giving orders as he bestowed his load. Hammers and drills, and a canteen of water, and a spoon to clean out the holes; until at last down the canyon the voices receded and Horse-Ketchum crept out of his hole.

If he stayed inside the gateway until the fatal shots were fired he would be caged up in that canyon with a madman—and Frying-pan George would shoot! Yet how could he escape, how find a way out with the old man guarding the entrance? Dusk was gathering in the deep valley, but high up on the eastern walls he could see the glow of the sun. In a hole like that, walled in by towering cliffs, there was no way out but one. Slowly and painfully he started down the path towards the entrance, but his strength was too far spent and he crept back to the crystal cave.

Evening came and the bats one by one fluttered past him on their way to hunt for gnats. They alone could escape from this abyss among the peaks. But if Horse-Ketchum gained the open he would be no better off, for the Night Riders would be watching the gateway. They had located the hiding-place of Frying-pan George, the source of his mysterious ore; and the specimen of gold-rock which they had taken from Horse-Ketchum would add new fuel to their greed. It was Breyfogle ore, and they knew for themselves now that Frying-pan's ore was the same. What to them were the golden horses which they had come to catch? The greatest treasure of Death Valley had been suddenly revealed to them and they would watch the canyon night and day.

Horse-Ketchum stretched out wearily behind his barricade of pack-saddles, well content with the poor comfort of a canteen of water and a sack of jerked meat and bread. He was safe within his cave, with Diana to care for him. And when his strength came back he could ride.

He was roused up at dawn by the resonant voice of Morgan as he returned to the cave below. Then the smell of smoke came to him and the incense of roasting coffee, but Diana did not appear. Hours passed and he gnawed hungrily at the sticks of dried meat, and when the foxes appeared at the mouth of the cave he did not respond to their wiles.

First one and then the other would creep a little closer, crouching down expectantly, wagging their bushy tails like dogs, yapping and chattering as they sniffed the meat.

"Here!" he said at last, holding out a sliver of jerky. And after watching him in silence the bolder of the two reached out and snatched it away. They were tame, as tame as dogs, and though his food was running low, Horse-Ketchum tolled them on with more and more. It served to while away the time and lighten the tedium of his confinement—to break in on his anxious thoughts. The foxes were sitting before him, their black-tipped noses out, when a head appeared in the doorway. Then swiftly Diana came gliding into the cave, and Johnny could see she was pleased.

In the dim light of the cave her eyes beamed on him approvingly as she passed him a pannikin of food, but she touched her lips for silence. Then she sat down, watching him as he poured out the hot coffee—meanwhile holding the pet foxes in her lap. But at a sound outside the entrance she leapt up like a flash, and Lightfoot was left alone.

Evening came and the fretful voice of the old man rose up as he called for his powder and tools. Perhaps that very night he would make good his threat and blast down the walls of the gateway. Horse-Ketchum listened anxiously as their voices died away; and then, despite his stiffness, he crawled out of his cave and slipped away up the trail.

A strong fence, with a stile, blocked the canyon from wall to wall; and beyond it, along the creek-bed, there was an irrigated garden, with corn and beans and cabbages in orderly rows. Then the canyon opened out into a broad valley among the peaks, a valley dotted with mesquite trees among which he could see the horses, reaching up to browse on the tips. Feed was short already, and not for many a moon would they graze on the salt meadows of Toógahboth.

Lightfoot climbed over the stile and sat down inside the fence to look out the rimrock for a pass. It rose sheer to the south, and the waning light of day showed frowning ramparts of black to the east. But the north wall of the valley was more broken, with streaks of white, and a trail ran along its base. He hobbled up it, bent over like an old man with the ache of his wounded back; and around the first point he came suddenly upon a canyon which split the wall in twain.

There was a path, worn deep, winding up among the boulders and over broken ledges of quartz; and on the further hillside, like a gopher-mound, a dump of rock had been thrown out. Horse-Ketchum quickened his pace. In such a place as this, with white quartz and limestone and a por-phyry contact on the east—in such a place gold might be found. And the dump showed that mining had been done. A sudden thrill went over him as, trampled in the dust, he saw the greasy wrapper of a powder-stick. Then at a turn of the trail he beheld a black tunnel with a big dump of waste at its mouth.

His knees, which had been so weak, suddenly regained their strength. He ran forward and stared into the hole, which smelled of dead powder fumes and sweat. In a pile by the entrance there was a heap of picked ore, and he knelt down trembling to examine it.

"It's gold!" he cried, snatching up a chunk of rock. "By the gods, it's Frying-pan's mine!"

CHAPTER XIV

MOON MADNESS

WITH a piece of gold quartz still clutched in his hand, panting and groaning with the weight of his pain, Horse-Ketchum hurried back to the mouth of his cave, stooping low like a man that hides. He had found the mine which Frying-pan George had kept hidden for twenty years. The Lost Breyfogle Mine! But what good was it to him, who sought only a way to escape? Yet he clung to the ore, with its pin-points of gold, and as he sank down he held it to his eyes.

Yes, imbedded in its matrix of blackened quartz, the mother of all evil gazed out at him with a pure and steady glow. It was the Breyfogle ore, for which for twenty years desert prospectors had sought and died. His heart leapt as he realized what wealth lay hidden here in this canyon with the one, guarded gate. And he had thought Diana's father crazy! But to hold a mine like that many a man would live as he had, shut away from all the world.

Horse-Ketchum sat dreaming, oblivious of the shadows which the moon cast among the trees; until, before his eyes, a shadow rose up and the moon-maiden stood before him. But the buckskin suit was gone and in its place she wore a dress, long and sweeping and gracefully draped.

"Were you waiting for me?" she asked as he sat staring in astonishment. And Johnny forgot his dreams. Her voice was so eager, her manner so sweet, her desire to please so apparent.

"Sure was!" he answered gallantly. "But, I declare, I hardly knew you. You're just like a lady out of a book."

"Like Maid Marion or Rebecca, or the Lady of Shalott?" she mocked. "I've read about them— over and over. But they all lived so long ago. What is the world like, now? Do the women wear dresses like these?"

"Nope, not nearly so handsome," he responded admiringly. "You sure look fine, now—Diana!"

"Oh, thank you," she replied with a curtsy. "This is one my mother made. She used to send out when Father went for supplies and order the most beautiful things! But now that she's gone all he brings me is calico—the kind they sell to squaws."

"Well, sit down," he invited, "if it won't get your dress dirty. And say, Diana—what's he doing down there? Is he going to shoot those rocks down tonight?"

"Oh, no," she answered lightly, "not for two or three nights. Perhaps he won't do it at all. There's something about the full moon that seems to make him worse. But now that he's slept he's better."

"You mean he don't cuss and cave around the way he did? No fooling—he had me scared. Are you dead sure he won't come up here and find us together, and fill me full of holes?"

"I'm not sure of anything," she sighed, gathering her skirt up and sinking to the ground. "But I thought, while you *were* here, I'd like to put this dress on and pretend to be a lady again. My mother was a Chatfield, one of the oldest Kentucky families; and every day, while Father was working in his mine, she'd instruct me in the ways of society. When I was sixteen years old she made me this silk dress—for my coming-out party, or début. But I've had it four years, and you're the first young man that I've had the pleasure to meet."

"The pleasure is all mine," responded Horse-Ketchum politely. "And if it wasn't for that charge of buckshot in my back I'd rise up and make my bow."

"Oh, dear!" she cried. "And I haven't looked at it all day! Did you keep the cloth wet with arnica?"

"Yes, and kept right still," he answered. "I reckon it'll soon be well."

"I'm sorry," she began hastily, "that I spoke the way I did—about horse-thieves and all the rest. But I'm a Morgan, I reckon, and Mother used to say they were all a hot-tempered lot."

"That's all right," mumbled Lightfoot. "Mighty glad you came back. I was afraid I'd lost you for good."

"Well, I *was* huffed," she confessed, "but when I looked in and saw you feeding my foxes I knew we just hadn't understood. I'm hotheaded, and so are you. But I'm not angry now. Will you shake hands? And let's be friends!"

"Suits me!"replied Johnny, reaching out his grimy paw. "And I'm sorry for what I said. But I was so badly scared your old man would bust in on us—and maybe have a killing, right there—that I didn't care *what* I said."

"I knew it," she nodded, "afterwards. And I knew you were not a horse-thief. You just thought our horses were wild."

"Sure!" assented Horse-Ketchum. "There wasn't a mark on 'em. And the law is, any horse that's running without a brand belongs to the first man that ropes him. But that Paynim-horse!" he sighed. "I took a big chance—and I'd take a big chance again."

"How big?" she asked, after a meditative silence. And Johnny saw her breast heave expectantly.

"A big one," he repeated. "But don't you worry, Diana. I won't ride him off, when I go."

"Oh, of course not," she murmured. "I didn't mean that. But why don't you stay here, Johnny?"

"What, and have your father find me, hiding out in that cave, and shoot me like a holed-up coyote? That's just what he'll do, and I know it!"

"Oh, no!" she protested feebly. "But—well, maybe you're right. Only, Johnny, couldn't you take me, when you go?"

A hush fell as he met her gaze in the moonlight—her eyes were as innocent as a child's. But she was a woman—a woman grown—and the world would not understand.

"If you could," she pleaded as he hesitated, "if you would—before he shuts us in! Then you could ride Paynim, and I would ride Moonbeam. And Paynim would always be yours! I would talk to him and tell him that you were his new master, and he'd follow you like a dog. Oh, couldn't you take me, Johnny? I'm afraid here, all alone!"

"No," he decided. "Your old man would kill me. If it wasn't for him, now! Well, maybe I'll come back—but I can't take you with me, Diana."

"But why?" she asked, after a silence. And Horse-Ketchum took her hand.

"Diana," he said, "I'd sure like to do it. With you and old Paynim—and Moonbeam, too! But no, it can't be done. You don't know the people outside. People like Hanks, and Val Bodie. Didn't your mother ever tell you to always think what people might say, and not take a chance with strangers?"

"Why, no!" she answered wonderingly. "She told me always to be good, and to do only what was right. But there weren't any people, you know."

"Well, I'll have to tell you, then," replied Johnny bluntly, "that people are a mighty tough lot. And they always think the worst. Where the devil would I take you if we got away alive? Have you got any folks in these parts?"

"My folks are in Kentucky," she responded. "But my father is hiding from them all. I don't know why it is, but the Chatfields and the Tollivers have fought each other for years. It was a feud, and my father was compelled to kill a man. So he came out here to hide."

"You bet!" agreed Lightfoot. "I understand all that. Those Kentucky mountaineers are always fighting each other. And I've heard about the Chatfields, too."

"He killed six of them," she went on steadily, "and then he started west. It was Mother that persuaded him to go. Her family were Chatfields, but she just couldn't stand it, to see her husband drawn into it. So he sold out his business and everything he had and they joined an emigrant train west. But his horses he wouldn't sell—they were just like children to him—and he took the four thoroughbreds along. Old Selim is living still."

"Sure enough?" exclaimed Johnny. "Are they genuine Kentucky thoroughbreds? But how did you folks get *here?*"

"I don't know," she answered pensively. "Father and Mother refused to talk about it. But one time he showed me from the top of the high cliff the spot where the emigrants all died. It is over at the base of that big, black mountain—and his folks, of course, believe him dead. But he escaped to this canyon, after a fight with the Indians. And when he found his mine Mother was willing to stay here, because the Tollivers would never quit looking for him. But before she died she told me Father was queer and it was better perhaps to go."

"Yes, but where to?" asked the practical Horse-Ketchum. "I'm game to take you out, if you've got any folks—"

"Listen, Johnny," she appealed, moving closer and gazing up at him, "I haven't got a kinswoman in the world. But I can ride as well as you can—I've rode all my life—and I'm not afraid any more. When I saw you first you looked so terrible, all covered with blood and dirt. But Paynim stood right over you and I knew you had been kind to him—that's why I brought you here. And then Christopher and Columbus, my dear little foxes, went right up and fed out of your hand. So I know you're a good man and I'm willing to go any-where, if you'll only take me away."

She laid her head on his shoulder and leaned against him expectantly, and Horse-Ketchum put out his arm. She was a child, he told himself, and held her close as he pondered an answer; but she turned and kissed him quickly on the cheek.

"I knew you'd hold me," she sighed. "No one does it any more, since Mother passed away. You can kiss me, too, if you wish."

She raised her lips impulsively but Horse-Ketchum dodged away.

"Hold on, now," he laughed. "Isn't this getting pretty familiar, considering our short acquaintance? How old are you Diana, anyway?"

"I'm old enough," she answered, "to have my own way. Are you going to take me with you when you go?"

"W'y, sure," responded Johnny lightly. "But what's that got to do with kissing?"

"It's got everything!" she declared. And before Horse-Ketchum could resist she had drawn him into a clinging embrace. "I just love you!" she breathed, and as her lips met his, Johnny forgot duty and danger and everything.

"That's good," he said, and kissed her again, before he put her reluctantly away. The glamorous moonlight had played him a trick—or perhaps it was Diana's kiss—for now he thought no longer of gold and a swift escape. He was content, like the Lotus-eaters, to dream.

CHAPTER XV

THE PROMISE

ON his couch within the cave Horse-Ketchum tossed and groaned, for his wounds pained the more as they healed. But while he lay in the black silence he remembered, like a phantasy, Diana sitting in the moonlight. Diana in clinging silk, with the moonshine in her hair and God's own innocence in her eyes. Diana like a child, creeping into his arms—Diana demanding to be kissed. He turned on his bed and moaned. Then sleep came and he awoke to a shadow hovering over him, and outside the cave it was day.

In the gloom of the cave he saw her, smiling anxiously, moving softly as she set down her tray. But as she stooped down he closed his eyes. He was weak, and he had forgotten the stern words he wished to say, to protect her from herself. Perhaps she would go away. He stirred, and swiftly across his brow he felt the touch of her hair. Then her cool cheek pressed his, there was the ghost of a kiss, and she laughed as he opened his eyes.

"It is late," she whispered, "and Father is asleep. Those terrible men have gone!"

"They'll be back," he grumbled. "I know that Bodie gang. They'll get up this canyon, yet."

"No they won't!" she retorted, beginning to wash

his grimy hands. "My father has expected this to happen for years, and he's got his plans all made. At the foot of the waterfall, where we climbed up that night, he has drilled deep holes in the bedrock. One blast will blow it out and leave a solid wall of stone, twenty or thirty feet high, at the least."

"They'll fill it up with rocks," predicted Lightfoot. "Or put up a ladder, some night."

"Yes—and then," she cried triumphantly, "he'll set off his big blast and blow the south wall down on top of them. It's hundreds of feet high and split from top to bottom. Only think if it ever came down!"

"My Lord!" exclaimed Johnny, "has he loaded his holes yet? Say, Diana—just look at my back."

"No, only the bottom ones," she soothed. "Oh, dear—you've hurt it again!"

"Never mind," answered Horse-Ketchum. "There's one thing dead certain. I'm going to get out of this canyon before he touches off them blasts!"

"Then you must lie still, and be quiet," she admonished, "and not go off, the way you did last night. I found your tracks up the canyon, where you went to the mine. Big foot-tracks! But I wiped them out."

"Yes—looking for some trail, to get out of here," he explained. But Diana glanced at him shrewdly.

"If Father sees one track around his mine—" she began.

"I know," nodded Johnny. "He'll kill me."

"He'll think you're trying to steal it," she ended anxiously. "And oh dear, I'm so afraid! But I've got it all planned, and here's some gold we can take with us. I picked it up, down in the creek."

She passed over a buckskin sack and Johnny forgot his qualms as he felt the weight of the gold.

"Gawd A'mighty!" he breathed, "can you pick it up like that?"

"Here's a piece I brought for you," she answered, and dropped a big nugget into his hand. Then she smiled and rattled on, while he listened in stunned silence, absently hefting the weight of the gold.

"I was so excited last night, I couldn't sleep a wink; but Father didn't come home. I hate to run off and leave him—and who'd feed my dear foxes? Poor Christopher and Columbus, I love them so much! And all the horses, too. We used to have such fun, down on the lake-bed at night. They all know their names—I raised them from colts. But there was nobody here to talk to. Poor Father—all he thinks of is his mine."

"Is it rich?" asked Lightfoot guardedly. "And say, what does he do with the ore?"

"Oh, he pounds it out in those Indian pot-holes, where they used to grind up mesquite beans. And then he washes it out in the creek-bed and puts it in buckskin sacks. It's beautiful up here in the spring-time, when the pussy-willows and mesquite trees are in flower. Could you stand it to live here, Johnny?"

"Not me!" declared Horse-Ketchum. "This canyon is too small. I like to ramble around, ketching horses and prospecting, and matching a race with old High Behind."

"But, oh think!" she exclaimed, "how *Paynim* can run! He can beat any horse in the world. When Father let them out, to feed down below, I used to run away—every night. When he was asleep I'd take Moonbeam and ride after them. With Christopher and Columbus, too! And we'd play on the lake until the foxes were tired out—and then we'd all race home. But now that Val Bodie has found where we live—do you think he's out there, Johnny?"

"You bet your life!" asserted Lightfoot. "And that's one thing I'm afraid of. If I take you out with me, like I promised last night—"

"Oh, but Johnny!" she cried, clutching his hand, "you *must* take me! Think of being shut in here—with him!"

"Yes, and think of being caught by that big, fat Val Bodie—and me, maybe, too weak to ride!"

"But I'd be on Moonbeam!" she protested. "And nobody could catch me—on her!"

"They caught you once!" he returned. "And say, where's my guns? Did you find them, down where I fell?"

"I saw them," she confessed, "a pistol and a rifle. But you're so heavy, Johnny—and after I'd lifted you up I just rode away without them."

"I see," he nodded, and lay in deep thought as she drenched his back with arnica. The danger from his wounds was past, but they stiffened him and impeded his movements. And after a short ride he would weaken, especially if it came to a chase. Yet any night now a fresh battle might spring up, or the mouth of the narrow canyon be closed. There was danger in delay—but even more in a flight, unless he could ride and shoot.

"Diana," he said at last, "I've got to have a gun. And a couple of six-shooters, too. Can't you get them from your father?"

"Yes, I could," she said. "But he takes them all with him. And the minute he missed one—"

"Well, just before I go, then," he assented. "I'll slip off while he's asleep."

"What? And not take me?" she gasped.

"I'll take you," he answered, "if you hold me to my promise—though how I ever came to make it is sure a mystery to me. You'd be lots safer here, Pet—and I swear I'll come back for you—"

"Yes, but when you took his guns—and maybe Paynim, too—"

"That's right," sighed Horse-Ketchum. "Well, I'll wait a while, Diana. And when I do go—"

"You'll take me!" she smiled. And before Johnny knew it she had kissed him and danced away.

CHAPTER XVI

A BROKEN DREAM

THERE was something disconcerting, and even a trifle suspicious, about the way Diana put promises in Johnny's mouth and then stopped his lips with kisses. They were childish kisses, of course, but at the second occurrence Horse-Ketchum began to have his doubts. All her life, so she said, she had lived within the portals of that gateway of solid stone. And yet, somewhere, in some way, she had learned to coax and wheedle and turn men from their purpose.

Better by far for both of them, with Val Bodie lingering near, if Lightfoot should slip out alone. Either afoot or horse-back he could travel and fight better—but Diana had had her way. And perhaps, he mused, her way would prove best. Every day brought back his strength, and from the cliff above she could watch for Bodie and his gang. Johnny settled down comfortably, clean and fed and with new-bound wounds, and the memory of her soft hands seemed to soothe him to sleep. When he awoke the day had passed, and Morgan was shouting below.

"Where have you been?" he demanded imperiously. And in the hush of evening Horse-Ketchum could hear Diana answer him.

"I've been up on the cliff," she called, "and Val Bodie is coming back. There are twenty-two men and eight packs, and they're riding up the valley towards Night Water."

"Well, come down here!" yelled her father, "and put me up some grub. Those rascals are determined to force their way up this canyon. But I'll show them, the cowardly whelps! I'll camp at the portals and give them a warm welcome if they come within range of my rifle. They think they can intimidate me, or creep in at night and murder me in my sleep. There's no doubt in my mind—they've come to kill us both in order to get possession of my mine."

His deep roar was muffled as he passed into his cave to get together his outfit and guns. But he came out, still cursing; and, Diana doing pack-duty, they passed out of hearing down the canyon. Horse-Ketchum rose up and crept out of his cave—he felt caged, like a rat in a trap. Sooner or later, if he stayed there, the old man would find his hiding-place; and then, without a gun, Johnny would be at his mercy. It was a sorry death to die.

The last rays of the dying sun painted the funereal cliffs blood red and an owl woke the echoes with his call. Night birds dipped down near him in the gloom of the canyon and the bats flitted noiselessly past. It was a grim, spooky spot, but along the pasture fence the golden horses stood nickering, their heads in an eager row. They had come to the stile when they heard their master's voice, but in the hurry their begging had been forgotten.

Johnny watched as bold Paynim thrust his head beyond the rest, and then he hobbled towards him. His back was healing now, but at each forward stride the stiffened muscles seemed to creak. Yet here was the horse that had saved his life and he took him his last piece of bread. Paynim reached for it delicately, with his lips and not his teeth, and as Johnny bestowed his peace-offering the horse suffered him to stroke his nose.

"By the gods," exclaimed Horse-Ketchum, "you're the top-horse of the world, Paynim! And a thoroughbred, eh, from Kentucky? You wait till my back is well and we'll ride out of this hell-hole!" But Paynim shook his head and turned away.

Not for one crust of bread and a pat on the nose would he let this strange horseman buy his friendship. He remembered the bite of a rope as it settled about his neck, the smashing fall, and the smothering hackamore. Then the long stubborn fight as he was led away from his mates and his last, frenzied battle for freedom. But back at the water-hole, ruthlessly, tied to a stake and left to swelter in the heat, he had seen this same enemy ride in and cut him loose and lead him back towards his canyon. It was for that—and the drink of water when he stood tied near the creek—that Paynim had amended his views. But he was a thoroughbred, and not easily won.

The two foxes trotted up as Johnny sat on the stile, wagging their tails but sniffing at him dubiously; and then, down the trail, he saw Diana coming back—and the horses all crowded to the bars.

"No, Moonbeam," she said, as she saw their eager heads, "we can never go back to Night Water. No, Paynim—no, Turco! Those bad men have come back!" And she reached up to pat Paynim's neck.

"They have come to stay, this time," she went on, turning to Johnny. "Val Bodie and all his men!"

"We're bottled up, then," he shrugged. "Isn't there any way out? Can't we find some trail up that cliff?"

"Only a mountain sheep can scale it," she responded. "And sometimes they slip and fall. When they come down to the spring Father shoots them for jerked meat, and I know every path they use. We're shut in, Johnny—are you mad?"

She sat down beside him and took one of his hands in hers while she leaned her yellow head against his. It was a way she had, and not for the world would Horse-Ketchum have it otherwise.

"I'm not mad unless you are," he answered gallantly. "We've got lots of company, anyway."

"Who do you mean?" she asked at last.

"Why, I've got you—and you've got me!" he said. And Diana tried to kiss him.

"Isn't it wonderful!" she breathed. "I'm so happy

it just hurts. If you'd been a bad man I don't know what I'd done. You're the very first one—and I love you!"

"That's good—that's fine!" he praised. "Only don't try to make me a pet. I'm kind of wild, you know, like an antelope. And if you pet 'em too much, they die."

"Yes. I know it," she answered gravely. "Or at least little mountain sheep do. But what do you really mean, Johnny? Don't you like to have me kiss you?"

"Oh, yes," he answered bluffly. "But you see it's this way, Diana—I never had a girl. And so I ain't used to being kissed."

"Well, neither am I—any more," she sighed. "But Mother used to kiss me, all the time."

"Poor little girl," he said. And she cuddled down into his arms, while the foxes crept close to her side. The moon, past its full, cast a pale glow on the canyon walls and the horses shuffled dejectedly away. Even the foxes fell to playing and disappeared among the shadows, but Diana did not stir.

"It's so long," she said at last, "since anybody cared for me. Have you got a mother, Johnny?"

"I've got nothing," returned Lightfoot, "except the horse I ride. And now I haven't even got a horse."

"Yes you have!" she asserted. "You've got Paynim, if you want him. Let's get your saddle and let him become used to it. I always ride them bare-back, you know."

"I can ride 'em that way, too," replied Horse-Ketchum. "But I'd sure like to mount him—just once. You don't reckon your old man will be back?"

"No, he's watching the gateway," she answered, skipping away. And she returned with the saddle on her arm.

"Here, Paynim!" she called, as she lowered the top bars and swung up over the rest. "They're jumpers," she explained, as she sat waiting in the moonlight. "We had to make the bars ten high. Oh, here he comes! Here, Paynim! And here's my Moonbeam, too! No, you can't go out the gate!"

She pushed their heads away as they leaned over the peeled poles and slipped a hair *macate* on Paynim.

"Now, here's your horse, Johnny!" she said, leading him over. "And Paynim, here's your master! Understand?"

She patted him on the neck as he snorted and drew back.

"No, Paynim," she commanded. "Now you stand! And Johnny, you put on your saddle."

Slowly and quietly, while his heart beat high, Horse-Ketchum fastened the cinch. Then at a word from Diana, he swung up into the saddle and took the end of the rope.

"Here, Moonbeam!" she summoned. And when

the mare came trotting up she mounted with a light, graceful leap. The two horses started off at a swift, rhythmic trot—they cantered, they galloped, they stopped. Even though his back was wounded, Johnny hardly felt a pang. It was the poetry of motion—it was speed! They turned and rode back, down the broad, level trail that the horses had worn to the gate; and then, in full flight, Diana swung over behind him and leapt back as Moonbeam swept past.

"Isn't it wonderful!" she sighed as they reined in at the gate, and Johnny patted his horse. His horse—the noble Paynim, whose sires for thousands of years had ranged the desert sands of Araby! He stepped off and dropped the rope and Paynim stood like a statue, head high, his sensitive ears intent.

"He hears something," began Johnny; and then, around his neck, he felt Diana's soft, clinging arms.

"He is waiting," she said; and at the touch of her body Horse-Ketchum felt a strange, wild thrill. She was panting from her exertion, her breath was warm on his cheek, and she drew his head slowly down. Then as she raised her upturned lips he crushed them with kisses, holding her close, like a fluttering, ecstatic bird.

"Oh, Johnny!" she gasped. "It's been so lonely, without you. Without anybody that I could love. Do you mind?" And she kissed him again.

A madness came over him—his brain reeled, his heart beat high. But as he held her, trembling, Paynim snorted and stepped back, and Horse-Ketchum raised his eyes.

Across the top of the stile a long gun was moving towards him, its muzzle pointing straight at his head. And behind it, his face contorted, stood Frying-pan George. Johnny ducked—and the gun went off. Then he ran, stunned and deafened by the thunder of the rifle; ran and dodged, and the gun roared again. But Diana had leapt forward and struck the barrel up, and he heard her voice calling:

"Run!"

Horse-Ketchum glanced back and saw them grappling for the rifle. Then as he fled he came on Paynim, dragging his *macate* as he made off, and with one bound he pounced upon the rope.

"Whoa, Paynim!" he soothed as he fetched him up with a jerk. "Whoa, Pet!" And he leapt on his back.

The pasture lay before them, but there was only one escape and Johnny turned the stallion to the gate. He charged down on it, confidently, gathering his feet for the jump. He crouched and Horse-Ketchum leaned forward. They were over, skimming the bars like a bird in full flight, and Paynim went thundering on. A gun roared behind them, bullets smashed against the rocks; but Paynim had his head and the open trail called him. He rushed around the corner and was gone.

CHAPTER XVII

THE CATACLYSM

THROUGH black shadows and garish moon-light Paynim went at a gallop, down the trail he knew so well—the glad trail to Toógahboth, where he could drink, and gambol on the lake-bed. Or perhaps some new loyalty to the man who bestrode him steeled his gallant heart for the race. Perhaps he knew that death followed and that danger lay before him, and sniffed the battle from afar. It was bred in his blood to love the tumult and the shouting, the yells of fighting men as they charged, and he took the trail gloriously until, near the portals, he slowed down with a warning snort.

Horse-Ketchum had ridden free, the rope slack on Paynim's neck; but as a great patch of moonlight opened up through the gateway he reined in and looked about. Below him, a pit of blackness, lay the pool of the dry waterfall, where Morgan had set his deep blasts; and against the overhanging south wall he could see empty canisters strewn about. He had loaded his holes, and the shattered wall above seemed ready to fall at a touch. Lightfoot listened and looked back—then at a touch of the spurs Paynim stepped off down the steep slope.

There was no retreat, and with a good horse

under him Horse-Ketchum felt his courage return. He was stripped down to his spurs, his gun and pistols were gone; but once out in the open he was armed with more than guns. He had speed—he was mounted on Paynim! Where the moon cast deep shadows along the south bank of the wash the stallion trotted on, snorting softly. Then at a second and lower gateway, between banks of storm-borne boulders, he halted and snorted louder.

The open wash stretched before them, piled high on both sides with windrows of rocks and brush; and among them, moving slowly, Johnny could see a line of horsemen, advancing towards the gateway. He was cut off, and if he whipped out they would ride in and head him. Discretion here was the better part of valor—he reined over and took shelter behind a rock.

Out on the flat the riders had halted, the great sand-wash seemed empty; but as he waited Lightfoot saw a man's head bob up. They had dismounted and were coming up afoot. First one and then another showed his head as he passed, keeping hidden behind the cut-bank of the channel; and out on the desert Johnny could hear distant voices and the clack of iron-shod hoofs on the rocks. Val Bodie's men were scouting out the gateway, and soon the furtive forms came back. Then a long line of horsemen came stringing up the wash and Johnny laid his hand on Paynim's nose.

Lightfoot set himself and waited, but just before they reached him the leaders came to a halt. Others rode up from the rear—their muffled voices rose louder until at last Val Bodie spoke out.

"Oh, hell!" he cursed, "are *you* seeing ghosts, too? How do you know the old codger is there?"

"I heard him!" defended a voice. "When I first went up there. I heard his horse coming—down the trail at a gallop—"

"Well, Hank, you go up there!" ordered Bodie. "And don't come back till you know something. He can't shoot to kill in this moonlight—"

"Oh, he can't eh?" sneered Hank. "Well, *you* try him. I've been up there and seen his work—he's drilling holes under that gateway and loading them with dynamite. He's trying to toll us in so he can shoot the wall down on us. I ain't lost no mine, at all!"

"Well, I have," retorted Bodie, "and I'm going to get it, too. It's the Lost Breyfogle—that's a cinch. There ain't no doubt that old Whiskers is Frying-pan George, and we know that he had the ore. Are you going to let one crazy old coon stand between you and a mountain of gold? He's shot two men already, so we'll be justified in shooting him and locating the mine for ourselves."

"I'm game to shoot him, all right," grumbled Boots. "What I'm skeered of is that *he* will shoot *me*. He done tried it, already, and come close enough—"

"Aw, shut up!" broke in Bodie. "Is there any man here that's got nerve enough to go up this canyon? If I have to do it myself I'll claim the whole mine. But the man that goes up there, gits half! The rest of you damned cow-thieves can go back to your knitting—I'll divide with the man that kills George!"

He paused, and in the silence that followed Johnny heard the sound of hoof-beats, up the canyon.

"There he comes!" yapped a voice. "That's the way he came before! Only now he's cussing to beat hell!"

"Shut up!" ordered Bodie, as the thunder of feet came nearer and Horse-Ketchum took a last look back. Diana's father was coming. Above the clatter of his horse Johnny could hear the old man cursing, and into a patch of moonlight he saw him ride at full gallop, his white beard whipping in the wind. But it was not to avenge his wrongs on Val Bodie that he came, and Lightfoot swung low on his horse. Then with a yell he dashed out, charging straight at the startled Night Riders, who scattered without firing a shot. But, though they gave way, they turned to look as he passed, and Bodie spurred after him on Fly.

"That's the stallion, boys!" he shouted. "Head him off! Don't let him out! By grab, there's a man on him! Ride!"

He fired his pistol into the air to warn the men

below, but the next moment a pandemonium of shooting broke loose as Morgan encountered the advance. Bullets were flying in every direction and horsemen went racing past; but Horse-Ketchum swept on down the wide, sandy wash, passing horsemen who stood confused and leading the pack of pursuers. One by one as he came upon them they reined out and gave him the trail, but when they heard the shouting and saw Bodie coming on Fly they jumped in and joined the chase.

Down the long, winding wash, over boulders and through bushes, Paynim led them like a stag before hounds; but they crowded their horses, whipping and spurring to cut him off, and Johnny slapped Paynim hard. A storm of gravel flew up behind as the stallion responded, and the Night Riders began to shoot. Then they came out on the lake-bed and with a glorious burst of speed the thoroughbred pulled out in the lead. Straight as an arrow he flew, his head splitting the wind, his mane and tail floating away, and Horse-Ketchum rose up, laughing.

The white playa seemed flying past him while he sat still on the back of his noble horse. The sound of his hoof-beats was like the rattle of a drum, drowning out the scattering pistol-shots behind. They were free, and all the horses that Johnny had ridden were forgotten in his love for Paynim. Even when his enemies were left far behind he let the stallion gallop on. There was nothing in the world but him and his mount, gliding out across a silvery sea.

A line of trees rose before him and Johnny turned to the south, down the trail that led out of the valley; while Paynim, blowing hard and shaking his head, slowed down to a gentle trot.

"Good boy!" exulted Horse-Ketchum, patting his neck again and again; and the foam-flecked stallion snorted forth his challenge as he gazed back into the night.

On the brow of the first hill Lightfoot stopped and listened. The rattle of rifle-shots came dimly through the night, and Paynim pricked his ears, but no one followed behind. Spits of light stabbed the blackness at the mouth of the canyon—they were fighting for their mountain of gold. Val Bodie and his Riders—and against them the half-crazed man known to them as Frying-pan George.

Horse-Ketchum sighed as he watched the distant fireflies that played about the mouth of Devil Canyon. But for Diana and her horse he would be shut in there yet, or run to earth like a rabbit. He had escaped, but Diana was lost. Not an hour before they had watched the moon's rising while she had demanded her kiss. Then Paynim had snorted and across the stile her father had risen up, shooting. Shots, races, pursuits had crowded one upon the other—new terrors, new dangers, new escapes—and now he stood alone on the floor of the mighty valley and looked back where the fire-flies played.

He was turning away to rub down Paynim's limbs when a flash lit up the sky. It was followed by a rumble and the deep thud of a blast. Then the canyon mouth was bathed anew in fire. It leapt up like the flare from the muzzle of a cannon, and there came a deep, earth-moving roar. The ground trembled again and with dull reverberations Horse-Ketchum heard the shattered wall fall. The gateway was closed—there was no way in or out. Diana was shut off from the world.

CHAPTER XVIII

A CHATFIELD

THERE was a low rumble in the air, the jostling of falling rocks as they came tumbling down from the shattered heights; and then with a last thump each found its lowest level and the desert stillness returned. Solemn mountains, rising high, made a black wall in the moonlight; and out across the flats Horse-Ketchum could hear the wild burros, stampeding before the noise of the blasts. Enúpi Gai had claimed its own. The Devil-man had struck and the canyon's mouth had closed like a trap.

Horse-Ketchum mounted and rode, his mind in a turmoil, hardly knowing which way he went; but at the entrance to the wash that led up to Daylight Spring, Paynim snorted and set his feet. Up that canyon, by Hole-in-the-Rock, as they rode out into the moonlight, twenty Night Riders had once swept down on them and led him back to Toógahboth, to be tied to a stake and starved. There was a menace in its dark shadows and Paynim drew back, turning his head down the Furnace Creek trail.

"What's the matter?" inquired Johnny, patting his neck solicitously. "Well, have your own way—that's a Jonah trail for both of us." And he reined away to the south.

The line of clay hills drew further away and giant sand-dunes loomed before them. Lost Valley fell behind and as dawn painted the east they came to Esahbwoó, the Place of Death. Paynim snorted and shied at the wreck of a huge wagon, rising up out of its covering of sand; and in the pale light of morning Lightfoot could see the marks of shovels, where others had been half unearthed. The treasure-hunters had been there, digging once more for the box of gold which legend said the emigrants had carried.

At the creek where Paynim's father, Selim, had given his master warning, Paynim snuffed the poison water and turned away. Then with his nose to the wind he followed the trail of the treasure-hunters, and Horse-Ketchum gave him his head. There was fresh blood on his shirt where the jumping and riding had opened his half-healed wounds, and his throat was parched with thirst. But Captain Jack had warned him of the poisonous qualities of the water and he spurred Paynim on towards the south.

Twenty miles down the valley, so Captain Jack had told him, there was a place called Enúpi Psoógobie, where a great stream of water gushed out. But they had avoided the spot, for the Shoshones often camped there, and Jack was a hunted man. He had stolen the daughter of Eatum-up Jake, the fiercest warrior of the tribe, and the penalty for his crime was death. But Captain Jack was waiting for his master at Pahrump, and Horse-Ketchum took the trail at a lope.

The sun rose, glaring, over the peaks of the Funeral Range and smote him with its torrid heat. Lightfoot found himself reeling as if from a blow and the wound on his head beat and throbbed. Then he caught at the saddle-horn, for he felt himself falling, but Paynim jogged steadily on. The spell passed and Johnny looked up to see strange mountains at his left; and at the base of a far hillside he spied a spot of green, with the white of a spring at its base.

Paynim raised his head as if he smelled the distant water and lengthened his jog to a lope. He was tireless as an antelope and before an hour had passed he was drinking at the drip of Cow Springs. Johnny dropped out of his saddle and buried his face in the muddied pool. Then he drank and wet his head, and while Paynim cropped the grass he lay in his shadow, to escape the burning sun.

The first hot day of summer had come and the valley lay quivering in the heat. Mesquite trees danced ghostlike in the close-up mirage; and below him, like a vision of some distant, desert scene, he saw the green tips of three palms. He rose up and watched them closely, and at their feet he saw a house—a white house, with trees behind. And along a picket fence a horse was plodding, an old horse with long, stilt-like legs. It was the mirage, of course, turning the desert into a lake and lengthening the trunks of the trees. But the horse was real—he moved!

Horse-Ketchum laid hold of his saddle-horn and heaved himself up on his mount, and as they jogged down the trail he could see a group of Indians, watching his progress from the top of a hill. Then at a turn of the path the house rose up before him, and a man was standing at the gate. Half-concealed behind a post, he held a rifle across his arm, and Johnny reined in to a walk.

"Hello!" he hailed, raising his hand in the peace-sign. But the stranger did not respond. He was watching him, intently, and as Lightfoot rode nearer he saw a woman, looking out through the door. A pretty woman, with black hair combed smoothly back; and she bore a baby in her arms.

"Who are you? And what's your business?"

demanded the man peremptorily. And Johnny came to a halt. Many times before in that wild, desert country where both fugitives and outlaws sought shelter, he had been met by men waiting at the gate. This man was tall and stooping, with high cheek-bones and level, piercing eyes—and Lightfoot knew he was on the dodge. Yet all he wanted was help.

"My name's Lightfoot," he announced. "Johnny Lightfoot, from Virginia City. I've had trouble, and I'm out of grub."

"Trouble with who?" inquired the stranger, after a pause. "We have to be careful, out here."

"With Val Bodie," responded Johnny. "He shot me in the back. We got tangled up over this horse."

"I've heard about you," nodded the man, beckoning him closer. "Is that one of those Night Water wild horses?"

"Sure is," answered Lightfoot. "But he's no more wild than I am. Look at that! He's gentle as a dog."

He dropped down off of Paynim and laid a hand on his nose, but the stallion did not flinch.

"Stranger, my name is Chatfield," spoke up the man behind the post. "Are you looking for anybody of that name?"

"Not me!" returned Horse-Ketchum. "All I want is a little grub. And I've got the money to pay for it."

"Well, come in, then!" invited Chatfield, throwing open the gate. "And I'm sure glad to see that horse. If you don't know it already I'll tell you right now—that's a thoroughbred Kentucky racer."

"I reckon you're right," agreed Johnny. "But that makes no difference. The horse is mine. I caught him."

"So I hear," responded Chatfield. "So the Indians tell me. But I had an uncle, Randolph Morgan, who perished up at Salt Creek, and I'll wager those horses were his."

"That was a long time ago," retorted Lightfoot. "Do you make any claim to this horse?"

"Oh, no," denied Chatfield, "but I knew Uncle Randoph's racers. Do you see those three black marks on the rump of this horse? Those are the direct, hereditary markings, come down from Eclipse, the greatest thoroughbred stallion in England."

Horse-Ketchum stopped short and brushed the hair out of his eyes, swollen half shut from riding bareheaded through the heat.

"Mr. Chatfield," he said slowly. "I don't give a damn for those markings or your uncle Randolph. If you want one of his horses, go and ketch him the way I did. This horse is mine, and I'll fight for him."

"You don't need to," answered Chatfield shortly. "I don't claim him, and never did. But it certainly is remarkable to find those black marks on a horse that's been foaled in Death Valley."

"Now, listen," flared up Lightfoot, "and get this

through your head, right now. It's the law in this country that you can't claim a horse unless he bears your brand. If a horse is running wild on the open range he belongs to the first man that ropes him. I roped this horse and I claim him, understand? It makes no difference where he came from!"

Chatfield gazed at him, glowering, his rifle in his hand; but before he could speak a woman's voice came to them—a gentle voice, but very firm.

"Jim," she said, "can't you see the man is sick? Don't keep him standing out in the sun!"

"No! Come in!" spoke up Chatfield. "And bring your horse in with you. Did you say Val Bodie shot you?"

"Four buckshot in my back. And bumped my head ketching this horse. He dragged me off in the rocks."

"Well, come in, come in!" invited Chatfield. "I'm sure glad Bodie didn't get your horse. He's a man I've got no use for, because I know he's a crook—and a cowardly, murdering crook at that!"

"Now, Jim!" warned the woman reprovingly. "Mr. Bodie never did us any harm."

"No, but he will," retorted Chatfield, "the first chance he gets. Well, alright!" And he led the way to the door. "Damaris," he said formally, "this is Mister—er—Lightfoot. Mrs. Chatfield—Mr. Lightfoot."

"Glad to meet you," mumbled Johnny, as she

146

came down the steps and smilingly offered her hand. "I'm a hard-looking case, but—"

"We'll take care of you," she said. And he felt her arm about him as he stumbled in through the doorway. Then in the coolness of the dark house his strength suddenly failed him and he sank down on a cot. He had traveled as far as his nerve could take him—far enough, for the woman was bending over him.

He awoke from a long sleep to hear a baby's thin wail and swift feet hurrying through the house. Then the voice of the woman as she took up her child, every word a cooing caress. It was strange, in this wild country—and with a husband like hers—but as Horse-Ketchum listened he smiled. But for her he would have stood bare-headed in the sun, until he fainted from weakness and pain. Now his bruised head was bandaged, a wet cloth lay over his eyes and he felt his strength coming back. But Chatfield was a fighter. He was hard.

Lightfoot took off the cloth and gazed about the room, and as he stirred Damaris' head appeared in the doorway and she tiptoed over to his side.

"How are you feeling?" she asked, running her hand over his brow. "Would you like a glass of cool milk?"

"You bet ye—gimme two of them!" responded Johnny. "I'm mighty nigh starved to death."

"Not too much at once," she advised him,

smiling, as she brought in a pitcher and a glass. "How did you happen to lose your hat?"

"I forget," he grinned, "whether Bodie shot it off or I lost it when my horse bumped my head. Sure needed it, too, this morning."

"It's getting hot," she said. "Nothing, though, to what it will be. It was a hundred and twenty-nine, last August."

"Lord A'mighty!" he exclaimed. "Were you here?"

"All summer," she sighed. "But the winters are wonderful. My husband has charge of the ranch."

"Ranch, eh?" he repeated. "What do you raise?"

"Oh, alfalfa—there's forty acres. And besides, he guards the water rights. The Borax Company claims the creek. But we're really here to hide— like all the rest of them, I guess. That's why Jim was a little sharp, at first."

"Oh, that's all right," responded Johnny. "You've more than made up for it. And my head was spinning like a top."

"I could see," she said, "your face going white. That's the way it affects them, before a stroke. So I just let you have a good sleep. But now, if you like, I'll get Jim and we'll doctor your back."

"Mighty kind of you," assented Horse-Ketchum. "Is my horse all right? Keep him tied, or he'll start back home."

"Yes, Jim has taken care of him," she answered and went out to call him in.

A blast of hot air, like the breath of a furnace, swept in as she opened the door; and Johnny could feel his head begin to spin. He had had a touch of heat. But as the door was closed a moist coolness rose up from the sprinkled earth of the floor. Despite the hot wind they kept their house comfortable—but what a place for a woman to live!

She came back, still smiling, and above her in saturnine calm her husband gazed down on their guest. He was over six feet tall, with the stoop of hard work in his powerful shoulders, but still a young man in his prime.

"Let me see your back," he said. And then with practiced hand he followed the course of each buckshot. "You're all right," he grunted. "No lead in you now. How many days ago were you shot?"

"Oh, four or five," ventured Johnny. "I've been hiding out in a cave."

"Mighty lucky," observed Chatfield, "to have that arnica with you. Damaris, fetch me out the balsam."

He cleaned up the wounds and poured on a fragrant balsam, that smelled of myrrh and aromatic herbs; but Horse-Ketchum knew from the grim silence he kept that his mind was still on the horse. Had he come here from Kentucky to seek the priceless thoroughbreds that his uncle had brought so far? Or was he too a fugitive from that terrible feud which had driven Randolph Morgan from his home?

Johnny meditated as he lay there, accepting favors from his hand, whether Chatfield had a claim on his horse. For Paynim was not a broomtail but a pedigreed stallion. And Lightfoot had taken him—nay, stolen him—from Morgan. But Randolph Morgan was buried from the world as surely as if he were dead. And for twenty years he had been counted dead, disguised as Frying-pan George. The horse was not Chatfield's, in any case, as long as his uncle still lived. He was Johnny's, to have and to hold until Devil Canyon gave up its living dead. And even then he would not be Chatfield's, for Diana was Morgan's daughter.

"Mr. Chatfield," he began at last. "What's this about your uncle? Did you come out here to look for his horses?"

"I came out here," replied Chatfield, "to get away from a feud. You might have heard of the Chatfield–Tolliver war. But the reason I came here, instead of somewhere else, was to find out the truth about my uncle. He was a man of wealth, and when he left the blue-grass country he took with him a box of money and jewels. These jewels, according to what I can learn from the Indians, have never been recovered from the wagons, which meantime have been buried by the sand. So at intervals I've been digging in the sand-dunes at Salt Creek—you might have noticed it when you came past."

"Yes, I did," admitted Lightfoot. "And I've

noticed something else. These Shoshones won't talk about that fight. They've got something on their conscience, because they looted those wagons. Maybe they've got the jewels hidden out."

"More than likely," grumbled Chatfield. "But seeing that wild stallion has settled my mind on one point. My Uncle Randolph died here. How many more horses are there up there?"

"Well—ten," answered Horse-Ketchum. "But there's no use of you hunting them. There ain't a horse in this country can ketch 'em."

"Then how did you ketch yours?" demanded Chatfield. And Lightfoot saw Damaris in the door.

"Well," he began, "it's quite a long story. But I roped him at the water-hole, by moonlight."

"Oh, Jim," spoke up his wife, "there's somebody coming. Panamint Tom is signaling from the hill."

For a moment Chatfield hesitated, eager to go on with his questioning. Then he rose up and grabbed his gun.

"It's Bodie," he said, after a long look out the door; and Johnny leapt up like a flash.

"Lend me a rifle," he clamored as he ran out on the porch. "He's after me—and my horse!"

"You don't need a rifle," answered Chatfield quietly. "You're our guest, Mr. Lightfoot—I'll attend to Val Bodie, myself."

He strode out to the gate and without a word of warning raised his gun to his shoulder and fired.

The bullet struck up the dust in front of a galloping horseman, and Horse-Ketchum recognized Bodie. He was mounted on Fly, and far down the road Johnny could see six other Night Riders. They had followed on his trail after their defeat at the gateway, wild with anger and the lust to kill. For once more, from under their noses, he had carried off the golden stallion and Bodie was out for revenge.

At the puff of dust he threw up one hand—but he came on, making the peace-sign. Once more, and with the same unhurried precision, Jim Chatfield raised his rifle, and the bullet struck almost at his feet. Bodie reined in abruptly, holding his hand up for a talk, turning to look back impatiently for his men; and as they spurred up behind him he jumped his horse into a gallop. But the big gun spoke again.

Bodie ducked as if he were shot and the men who rode behind him swung down along their horses' necks. Then they stopped and Bodie began to shout. But Chatfield, without listening, stepped out from behind his post and motioned them imperiously away. Bodie looked about wildly—at the Indians up on the hill and the lone man with a rifle on his arm. Then he reined away abruptly and galloped off down the road while Chatfield paced back to the house.

"I know jest how to handle that kind of folks," he said. "Learned it early, back home in Kaintuck."

CHAPTER XIX

FOR LITTLE JIM

JIM CHATFIELD," cried his wife, "what in the world do you mean, shooting at Bodie without making a sign? Haven't we had troubles enough without your beginning all over again and starting another feud?"

"Oh, sho, sho, now, Damaris," he replied good-naturedly as he shoved three more cartridges into his magazine. "It's all right—there's no harm done. If I'd let 'em come closer they'd've started a fight and then I'd had to kill someone. And if they had come to the gate they'd've demanded Mistuh Lightfoot; and I wouldn't give him up, nohow."

"I sure want to thank you, Mr. Chatfield," spoke up Horse-Ketchum. "Because there's no doubt they had come to get me. But I certainly hope," he added, with a glance at Damaris, "that I haven't brought down trouble on your home."

"None in the world!" declared Chatfield with an easy smile. "This man Bodie has been pestering me and I'm right glad we had a show-down. Now he'll know right where to find me."

"Now, Jim," reproached his wife, "you know very well you just did that to start another war. I declare, it's in the blood. I never knew a Chatfield that wouldn't pick a fight, if he could!"

153

"The same to you," grinned Chatfield. "Ain't you a fighting Tolliver? I was sure a lucky man to win you for my wife, with that tribe of warriors on my trail."

He put his arm about her waist and drew her down beside him and now his hard face was suddenly illuminated by a kind and rugged smile.

"That's why I loved you so," he went on soothingly. "There's no coward blood in your veins. The Tollivers are all fighters, and I'm a fighter myself. When I tell a man to stop, he wants to stop."

"Yes, but Jim!" she sobbed. "You never made a sign. You never even lifted a hand. Think of our baby in there! And what would become of us if these ruffians of Bodie's should kill you?"

"They won't kill me," he answered confidently. "I never felt so safe in my life. Those Indians are better than watch-dogs, and no man can pass that gate without asking for my consent. And another thing, Sweetheart—I looked that gang over, and the man behind Bodie was Riley Sloper!"

"Riley Sloper!" she cried. "Oh, Jim, they've found us! They'll all come here now—the whole clan!"

"No they won't," he comforted. "It's too far away. I could have killed Riley; but, just for your sake, I sent the bullet past his ear."

"Oh, Jim!" she burst out, laying her head against his breast. "I'm afraid. Don't you go outside the fence!"

"No, I won't, darling," he promised. "Until the hot weather comes on. Then they'll all go away. The whole gang!"

"Oh, I wish it would get hot, then," she sighed. And Horse-Ketchum cleared his throat.

"Seems to me," he suggested, "not to contradict anybody, it's pretty near hot, already."

"You're not used to it," returned Chatfield, giving his wife a kiss and sending her into the house. "It's only jest beginning to get warm. Wait till the south wind blows up and the sand-storms come in and the water in the salt-marshes boils. Yes, suh, boils! I've seen it myself. And why shouldn't it, I'd like to ask, when it's a hundred and thirty in the shade and water boils at two hundred and twelve? There's only a few degrees difference—and the more salt you put into your water the quicker the pot will sing."

"Yes, but how do you live?" demanded Lightfoot.

"Oh, we live," shrugged Chatfield. "Lots of water, running right past. Come over here and I'll show you my fan. The old fly-wheel off of an engine—I run it by water-power. That's really what keeps us alive."

He led the way to a long corridor, between the two mud houses which were ensconsed beneath a double roof; and as he lifted a gate the rushing ditch was turned aside, sending its waters over a miniature mill-wheel. The flume filled, the paddles turned; and with a thrashing beat the fly-wheel started its fan. Splashing water wet the wings as they went whistling past, and down the narrow hallway a cool wind stirred the dust, until Chatfield sprinkled water on the floor.

"In front of that," he said, "with a wet sheet for a cover, you could outlive a blast from hell. And when people are hunted as Damaris and I have been, we're glad when the hot weather comes. Even the Shooshonnies quit us and go up on the peaks. We're alone, for months at a time. That's why we stay, here. We're safe."

Horse-Ketchum nodded silently, taking his stand in the cool draft that sucked down the dampened corridor, and Damaris came out of her room.

"*Here's* why we stay!" she smiled, holding up a cooing baby. "This is young Jim—James Tolliver Chatfield."

"I see," responded Johnny. "You've done called the feud off, eh?"

"Yes," nodded Jim. "But the Tollivers haven't. You see we couldn't be married, on account of the feud, so—"

"So he rode over and stole me," ended Damaris. And she cast a proud glance at her husband.

"Yes, I'll have to admit it," confessed Chatfield. "But I just had to have her, that's all."

"I've never regretted it," said Damaris. "How could I, with little Jim and all? But if Bodie should come back—"

"You can count on me!" spoke up Horse-Ketchum, impulsively. "I'm only one man, but if the kid here needs my services—"

He held out one finger and Little Jim laid hold of it, while his parents exchanged glances and smiled.

"I'll shake on that, too," announced Chatfield. And Damaris gave Lightfoot her hand.

"You took me in," said Johnny, "and I stay by my friends. But say, I've got something to tell you."

He sat down in the cool corridor and told them briefly of Randolph Morgan. And last of all he mentioned Diana.

"Oho!" exclaimed Chatfield. "So that's who took care of you while you were hiding out in that cave."

"Yes," admitted Lightfoot, "it was Diana who took care of me. And to tell you the truth, it was Diana who found me and smuggled me up the canyon. But when her old man discovered us—"

"You fell in love with her!" charged Damaris impulsively.

"Yes—and her father tried to kill me," responded Johnny. "I might as well tell you the whole of it."

"Oh, Jim!" she breathed, leaning her head against her husband and gazing up into his eyes. "Isn't it wonderful? Shut up all her life in that canyon, and then to have *him* come by! Was she afraid?" she demanded eagerly. "Why, she'd never even *seen* a young man!"

"Now, darling," protested her husband, "isn't this getting kinder personal?"

"No, that's all right," smiled Horse-Ketchum. "You folks are her cousins and you're entitled to know the truth. Diana was afraid—at first. But after we became acquainted—well, of course she'd been very lonely. And especially since her mother's death. Her father undoubtedly is insane."

"Yes, but why did he try to kill you?" persisted Damaris.

"Well, he found us together," answered Lightfoot, shortly. "Sitting out in the moonlight, watching the horses. We were up on the stile, and I'd just saddled Paynim—when I saw his rifle shoved out towards me. I ducked and it went off, right over my head, so there's no doubt about his intentions. But Diana grabbed the gun and I jumped Paynim over the bars—"

"So that's the way you got him!" spoke up Chatfield.

"That's the way!" agreed Johnny. "And if you want to call it stealing—"

"No, no—the horse is yours! But I thought you said at first—"

"I said I roped him," nodded Lightfoot. "And I did. I'm the first man to ketch one of those Night Water horses, but Val Bodie took him away from me. Then when I went down to steal him back Diana rode in on us and Bodie caught her horse, too. It would take all day to explain the rest of the mix-up. But when we got through I'd turned both horses loose and stopped a load of buckshot, to boot."

"And Diana escaped!" thrilled Damaris. "Then she found you and carried you home!"

"But unfortunately," continued Johnny, "her father had sworn that he'd kill the first man he caught there. He's got a rich mine and he's afraid somebody will steal it—"

"Oh! So *that's* why he tried to kill you?"

"Reckon so," grunted Horse-Ketchum. "Didn't stop to ask no questions. So here I am—horse and all."

"And are you planning," she asked roguishly, "to go back and rescue Diana? Uncle Randolph will be watching for you, now!"

"I didn't tell you," replied Lightfoot, "but right after I left he blew up the entrance to the canyon. Shot the walls down and closed the gateway—you could feel the blast for miles. So I'm afraid I can't get back."

"Why, Jim!" she cried. "Uncle Randolph *must* be crazy. "Can't you go up and help her, Honey?"

"You don't need to," interposed Johnny, "while I'm on the job. And if anyone can get her out, I can. But in case I do get in there and rescue Diana, can I count on you folks to take care of her? Because, to tell you the truth, she wanted to come out with me. Only of course there was no place to go."

"Why, certainly!" exclaimed Damaris. "Just think of the poor child, and no one but him to turn to! Is she pretty, Mr. Lightfoot? Is she? Honest?"

"She's too pretty," responded Johnny. "That's what I'm afraid of." And Damaris exchanged glances with her husband.

"Well, you bring her right here," she answered demurely. "And Mr. Lightfoot, you're a very nice man."

CHAPTER XX

CAPTAIN JACK

HORSE-KETCHUM awoke at daylight to hear a woman singing. It was Damaris, humming while she worked. The heat of the day had passed, and the long, sweltering night, and she was up about her tasks at dawn. What was it, he wondered, that made her heart so glad at the bottom of this sink-hole of hell? With death so near at hand, what had she to sing for? And yet as he listened she sang on.

Not for many a year had he heard a woman singing. There was something about her voice that reminded him of Diana, when she too had awakened to love. He had not forgotten the clinging touch of her arms, the childlike kisses on his cheeks, the raptures of delight with which she greeted him in the dusk. But it was her secret—he would guard it well. No one in the days to come, if he saved her from her imprisonment, should mention it to her shame. She was his, to take care of and protect.

He tiptoed out on the porch and looked back up the long road. But Val Bodie would be watching for him, now. Past the door, in a wide ditch, a brawling stream of water flowed down from the canyon above, and along its banks he could see the *rancheria* where the Shoshones made their camps. These were Captain Jack's people but they seemed to know Horse-Ketchum, for they avoided him, with sullen looks. Yet little that happened escaped their eyes—they were watching him now, from the distance.

Johnny felt of his lame back to see if he could ride and stumped out to Paynim's corral. Here at least the stallion was safe, for Chatfield had built a stockade of mesquite posts with no entrance but the gate in front. It surrounded his house like the outworks of a fort—and Jim too was up with the dawn. A forkful of hay came over the fence from the stack on the other side, but Paynim raised his head after he had seized the first mouthful and gazed at his master anxiously.

"No, Paynim," said Lightfoot, "we're not going home today. I've got to go to Pahrump and find my pet Indian; and you're too danged good-looking, old horse. You're like a pretty woman—you'd just get me into trouble." And he patted him on the neck.

"I'll stake you to a horse," shouted Chatfield over the fence. "And a good horse, too, Mr. Lightfoot. You just leave Paynim here, and when you go to Pahrump bring me back a box of cartridges."

"I'll bring you back ten boxes," promised Johnny, "if you'll keep Bodie from stealing Paynim." And that evening after dark he rode up Furnace Creek on Chatfield's rangy roan.

Hour after hour he kept on up the gravelly wash until, crossing the summit, he saw the pale quarter moon, rising belatedly over the desert. He was up out of the sink, on the broad reaches of the Amargosa, whose bitter waters in time of flood swept south of the Funeral Range and back into Death Valley itself. It was a country that Lightfoot knew, for Captain Jack had led him through it when they were hiding their trail from the Night Riders, and as daylight approached he rode in towards Shoshone, to take shelter in its thickets of mesquite. But as he circled the point and headed up towards the spring he came upon his own mule, feeding.

For a moment, despite its brand, Johnny doubted his own eyes. Yet here was his pack-mule, hobbled, and in the distance he could see Captain Jack's horse. He even recognized, among the mesquite trees, the top of his own tent. But he had told Jack to await him at Pahrump. Horse-Ketchum quit the trail and took cover among the screw beans, and as he spurred on his anger grew. While he had been fighting lone-handed against Bodie, Captain Jack, his Man Friday, had seized the occasion to decamp with his mules and supplies.

The tent was set back in the midst of the thicket at the end of a narrow path and when Lightfoot saw his coffee-pot on the stones of an Indian fire he reined in and drew his gun.

"Hello!" he hailed; and from the door of the tent a woman stared out at him, wondering. She was a Piute, and not uncomely, with a clean dress and her hair neatly banged. For an instant she stood at gaze. Then, seeing a white man, she dove under the tent and fled through the brush like a rabbit. Horse-Ketchum looked around at the old, familiar things—his butcher-knife, his hatchet, his rawhide kyacks—and at sight of his own bed spread out in the tent he let out a louder yell.

"Jack!" he shouted. "Where are you—you damned rascal? Come out of that brush! This is Horse-Ketchum!"

"Ho! H'lo!" responded a voice from the depth of the thicket; and Captain Jack gazed out at him, furtively.

"What the devil do you mean?" demanded Lightfoot indignantly, "running off with my outfit and mules? Come out of there, doggone it, or I'll shoot you!"

"No! No shootum!" protested Jack, stepping out into the open. "Wha's matter? Me thinkum you dead!"

Captain Jack was nattily attired in Horse-Ketchum's own cartridge-belt and his tailored town-pants. His blue shirt, his silk handkerchief—

only the wire-haired head and the startled, beady eyes kept the disguise from being complete. But Captain Jack was frightened—he was trembling.

"Ho! H'lo, there!" he greeted again, advancing with a doubtful smile. "You Horse-Ketchum? Where you been?"

"None of your danged business!" burst out Lightfoot angrily. "Why the hell didn't you go to Pahrump, like I told you? And you've sure got a nerve, putting on my best clothes. Doggone you, Jack, I ought to kill you!"

"No! No killum!" entreated the Indian apologetically. "Everybody say: Horse-Ketchum she dead. Me see Bodie, ride your horse. Me see Pete Boots, wear your hat. No come back—me thinkum dead."

"Like—hell!" railed Johnny. "Who's that woman that run away?"

"My wife!" announced Captain Jack. "Me ketchum 'nother woman. Piute woman—good squaw."

"Yes, but that don't give you license to give her my blankets and set her up in housekeeping in my tent. You can keep the outfit now and I'll buy me another one. How much of that money have you got left?"

"All gone!" answered Captain Jack dolefully.

"What? The whole five hundred? What'd you do with it, Jack? You owe me for this outfit, savvy?"

"Money gone!" repeated Jack. "Me buyum squaw—Ash Meadows. Good woman—he costum four horses. Then—well, buyum grub—givum feast.

Everybody git drunk. Pretty soon money all gone."

"Hell's—bells!" grumbled Horse-Ketchum, surveying his purloined outfit. "Well, Jack, you can work it out."

"No!" objected the Indian. "Me ketchum woman, now."

"No difference!" responded Johnny. "You stole my outfit—savvy? You know what the Hiko man does when he ketches an Indian stealing!"

He wrapped his finger around his neck and made a motion up and Captain Jack saw a new light.

"You go back—ketchum horse?" he inquired. "My wife, he go too. Good cook!"

"You send your wife home to her people," ordered Lightfoot. "Give her grub, give her blankets, give her everything you stole. But I don't want a woman along."

"Where you go?" repeated Captain Jack. "Too hot Death Valley now."

"Too hot for woman," answered Johnny grimly. "You send her back to Ash Meadows."

"Me 'fraid!" came out Jack. "Maybeso Shooshonnies kill me. Eatum-up Jake—she mad. Me buyum Piute woman. Shooshonnies all mad—maybe killum."

"Now here," said Horse-Ketchum, "I'll take care of the Shooshonnies. You're my Injun, savvy, and I need you in my business. I won't let anybody kill you."

"All right—me go," agreed Captain Jack. And

then he glanced up at him slyly. "You go back—ketchum horse?" he asked.

"No, Jack," grinned Johnny, "I'm going to steal me a woman. You come along and help, and when we get through—"

"What woman?" Jack demanded eagerly.

"Never mind," said Lightfoot. "You know the devil-man, at Night Water? Maybeso we steal his girl."

"*No wano*!" grunted Captain Jack. But Johnny regarded him sternly.

"I know what I want," he said. "You ain't called in on this at all, you old rascal. You know the ghost-maiden that used to ride the moon's horses? All right, we're going to steal her."

"No good!" repeated Captain Jack stubbornly; and then his sly grin returned. "How much you pay me?" he asked.

"I'll pay you one hundred dollars—and all this stuff you stole."

"All right," answered Jack. "Me go."

CHAPTER XXI

HORSE-KETCHUM PAYS RANSOM

THE trail to Mormon Lake was crowded with prospectors as Horse-Ketchum rode out of Pahrump. And the name on every lip, the magic word that lured them on, was Breyfogle. The Lost

Breyfogle had been found! He listened curiously, hardly believing his ears, to the rumors of the strike; and then it came over him that he himself had seen the treasure. The rush was to Devil Mountain.

As they neared Daylight Pass the stampede reached its height. Men threw away their blankets, their provisions, even their water-kegs, in order to be the first on the grounds. They traveled day and night, flailing their reluctant animals on; until, at Hole-in-the-Rock, they met the tide setting back, and all the rumors fell flat.

"It's a fake!" yelled the boomers as they came dragging into camp. "Go back, you damned fools, before you perish with the heat. It's another one of Bodie's snide tricks."

But the stampeders never wavered. They poured on down the canyon until they came to Night Water, where a hundred men were camped under the trees. And with them, leading the van, went Horse-Ketchum and his Indian, for Val Bodie had disappeared. He it was who had spread the rumors of treasure trove, showing the sacks of rich ore he had bought from Frying-pan George, exhibiting Johnny's Breyfogle rock. But when the leaders of the rush fought their way to Devil Mountain they found the entrance to the canyon blocked.

A wall of loose rock a hundred feet high dammed the way to the fabled bonanza, and up on the cliffs Frying-pan George was standing guard, ready to shoot any man who approached. It was then the rumor spread that Val Bodie had started the rush in order to bring trade to his store. Coming and going through Mormon Lake the stampeders had spent their money, with whisky at two-bits a drink; but when the first rumors of a fake sprang up Bodie had ridden off, no one knew where. All they knew was that with him he had taken the Breyfogle gold—and their gold, spent over the bar.

Horse-Ketchum camped at Night Water, where not a month before he had rescued Diana from the clutches of Bodie. Now she and her horses were shut up in the canyon, and across the entrance there was a wall of crumbling rock. Through his glasses he could see the raw scar along the cliff where the towering mass of stone had come down. But though he scanned the bench above, nothing stirred on the lookout point, and at sundown he rode up closer.

At the mouth of the canyon, blocks of rock had come tumbling down; but below them, where once the waterfall had been, there was a wall of solid stone. Randolph Morgan's first blast had shot out the inclined slope, and the second blast had brought down the cliff. There was no way up to the mass of shattered rock which hung at a balance above: and how could one hope to surmount that dizzy pile, where every piece seemed tottering to its fall?

Lightfoot stood in the gathering dusk and gazed

up at it grimly. Morgan was crazy, of course, but there was a method in his madness; for with two shots of powder he had shut his enemies out, and his horses and gold mine in. His cave was stored with provisions, the mountain sheep would supply his meat; and whenever he became weary of his complete isolation he could blast the canyon mouth clear. Johnny called, but no one answered and he went back to Night Water, where the stampeders had plans of their own.

Others had tried and failed; but in the morning they rode up to essay the solid barricade. Behind it lay the Breyfogle, greatest of all the storied mines which had made Death Valley famous; and as they lined up before it they discussed their scheme for blasting the obstruction away. Given the time and the powder, the canyon entrance could be cleared; but while they scanned the gateway Horse-Ketchum watched the heights, where Frying-pan George stood guard. A head appeared over the rampart and a gun-barrel flashed. Then, balanced fearlessly on the brow of the cliff, the old man waved his rifle.

"Get away from there, you scoundrels!" he bellowed. And like one man the stampeders obeyed. But as they spurred back out of range Johnny turned and watched the crags, waving his hand as a signal for Diana. Had he murdered her in his rage, this crack-brained old reprobate who stood menacing them still with his gun?

Lightfoot reined in and shouted her name, while the rest whipped away; but his only answer was a shot from the cliff. Morgan had recognized his enemy and sensed the errand that brought him there, for the bullets came thick and fast. But as the shooting began Johnny spied a silvery fox, running away over a pile of rocks. And beneath, peeping out from among the boulders, he saw Diana's golden head. Then a bullet came too close and his horse snorted and whirled. He waved his hat and fled, but his heart was glad. Diana lived, and she knew that her lover had come back for her. But he could not save her now. For to fetch her from that canyon, even if he could enter it, he would have to kill her father. It was better to wait, and come back.

All day the terrific heat beat down on their camp, while a wind out of the sink snatched up gravel and silt and buried them deep in sand. It came ladened with the stench of steaming marshes and of acrid, sun-smitten greasewood, a smell such as Horse-Ketchum had never sensed before—the rank breath of Death Valley in the heat. Wailing and grumbling while they waited for the sandstorm to lull, for the sun to sink at last behind the mountains, the prospectors at Night Water called down a thousand curses upon the author of their plight.

Val Bodie it was who, to gain a few dirty dollars, had brought them to this sink-hole of hell; but they swore, one and all, to raze his store to the ground if they ever escaped alive. So they lay, panting like lizards in the thin shade of the mesquite trees, until the long day came to a close; and as a cool night wind sucked in from the high ground Horse-Ketchum rode off with the rest. But where the others turned off towards Daylight Pass, Lightfoot kept on south towards Furnace Creek Ranch, where Jim Chatfield would be awaiting his aid.

Val Bodie was desperate now and, to avenge a fancied wrong, he was capable of any mischief. He held to the outlaws' code, and Jim Chatfield had humiliated him, turning him back before all his followers, whom so often he had rebuked for their faintheartedness. He had deprived him of his revenge when he had followed on Lightfoot's trail; and, more than that, he had deprived him of Paynim. It was that loss, most of all, which had roused Bodie's rancor, and Horse-Ketchum knew he would come back.

The Stygian gloom of a desert night had settled down over Death Valley, as if the darkness like a river had drained down into its black depths, making the trail invisible from a horse. Captain Jack rode in the lead, driving the pack-mules before him; Horse-Ketchum was deep in his thought; when on the salt-meadows by Esahbwoó, where the emigrants had perished, a horse neighed, loud and clear. Captain Jack's pony answered, the mules added their brays; and then out of the darkness, leaping and fighting against his hobbles, High Behind came crow-hopping up.

Horse-Ketchum knew him first, for he recognized his neigh, and before Captain Jack could stop him he swung down to cut him loose.

"Somebody come!" warned Jack as sudden voices were heard; and Lightfoot grabbed High Behind by the mane. Then, feeling his way down his fore legs, he slashed off the heavy hobbles and leapt up on Chatfield's horse.

"Who is that?" challenged a voice, and Jack turned the horses away. It was Val Bodie—he was digging out the wagons.

"Go to hell!" taunted Johnny, throwing High Behind into the bunch. And as Bodie began to shout they took the back trail at a gallop, then turned off and made for the hills. The black night swallowed them up and they halted in a swale as a band of horsemen loped north. Then quietly they headed south, with High Behind trotting free, and never stopped till they came to the ranch.

From the top of the lookout hill a high yell roused the house and brought Chatfield to the gate with his gun. But Lightfoot rode up laughing, reaching over to slap old High Behind, who responded with a playful kick. He had turned another trick on the unlucky Val Bodie and stolen back his captured horse. No small prize in itself, for High Behind was a racer and a range-toughened mustang, to boot.

"Look what I've got!" he called. "My old

mustang-chaser, High Behind—the horse that Bodie stole. And this is my Indian, Captain Jack."

"Drive 'em in," responded Chatfield. "And send your Injun up the ditch. I don't allow 'em inside the fence."

"Not any of 'em?" pleaded Lightfoot. "Jack's a mighty good Indian and—"

"No Injuns!" answered Chatfield shortly. And Captain Jack rolled his frightened eyes.

"No, but listen," began Johnny as he saw the Shoshones advancing in a body down the ditch. "My Indian has had trouble with Eatum-up Jake—"

"I don't give a damn!" broke in Chatfield harshly. "No Injun passes that gate. Understand?"

His face, which had been so friendly, was drawn down in angry lines and his jaw was set like a steel-trap.

"Yes! Sure I understand!" answered back Horse-Ketchum angrily. And he turned the horses back from the entrance.

"What's the matter?" cried Damaris, running down to the gate with Little Jim still in her arms. "Oh, Jim, Mr. Lightfoot is our friend!"

"I don't care!" flared back Chatfield. "He can't dictate to me. That's my rule. No Injuns inside the gate."

"Then I'll just camp outside!" answered Johnny. "Come on, Jack. And don't you be scared."

He rode around the pack-mules and drove them

173

over to a mesquite tree that stood on the bank of the ditch, and Captain Jack followed in a daze. First he glanced at his master, then at the crowd of jabbering Shoshones. But at sight of Panamint Tom, the war-chief, he dropped off and fell flat on the ground, with his hands up over his head. For he had stolen a Shoshone woman, and the punishment for his crime was death.

Panamint Tom strode over towards him, leaving the rabble behind, and gave him a kick in the ribs.

"This Shooshonnie country!" he said in English, for the benefit of Horse-Ketchum. "All this side of them mountains"—and he pointed to the Funeral Range—"Shooshonnie country! This Injun *Piute!*"

He grunted contemptuously and gave Jack another kick, but he only groveled down at his feet. Then in a long and impassioned speech, pointing often to the mountains and thrusting out his lips at Jack, the war-chief harangued his people. By the pantomime alone, and the few words he understood, Horse-Ketchum could follow the tale of Captain Jack's treachery to the tribe. He acted out the theft of the pretty Shoshone girl and as he went on to describe her distress and ultimate death shouts of anger went up from the crowd.

They were swart men, with high cheek-bones and the bold eyes of their forefathers, the warlike Shoshones of the north; but Panamint Tom himself stood head and shoulders above them all, and he advanced upon Captain Jack threateningly.

"*No wano!*" he declaimed, giving the culprit another buffet while he glanced first at Lightfoot and then at Chatfield. "Bad Injun—stealum woman. Shooshonnie people killum. *Me* killum!" And he reached for his knife. But Horse-Ketchum stepped to the front.

"This my Injun," he stated. "You leave him alone. I hired him to help me ketch horses."

He faced the Indians calmly, and once more Panamint Tom glanced over at the face of his boss. But Jim Chatfield stood grimly silent, though his wife was clinging to his arm, and the war-chief turned back arrogantly.

"This Shooshonnie country!" he said again, pointing his hand towards the eastern mountains. "Piute Injun come over—we killum. Shooshonnie go over—Piute killum." He nodded, and reached for his knife.

"Here! Now listen!" spoke up Horse-Ketchum with a good-natured smile. "This man is my Injun. Understand? Maybeso him Piute—maybeso him Shooshonnie. No difference. He works for me."

"*No wano!*" shouted the war-chief. "This man stealum woman. Good woman—b'long Eatum-up Jake!"

He waved his hand towards a gaunt and evil-eyed savage who had been yapping on the edge of the crowd, and with a yell of defiance Eatum-up Jake leapt forward, a long knife clutched in his hand. His drawn face was working fiercely and there was murder in his eye; but when Horse-Ketchum stepped towards him he stopped.

"Now here!" warned Lightfoot, and one hand touched his gun. "You put up that knife before my pistol goes off and another bad Injun bites the dust. You leave this man alone. Understand?"

"*No wano*!" shrilled Eatum-up Jake, making a futile kick at Jack. "She steal my girl. Me killum!"

"No you won't," contradicted Johnny, "do anything of the kind. How much you want for your girl?"

A subtle change came over the countenance of the outraged father, and he turned exultantly to the crowd. They shouted in great excitement and Eatum-up Jake shouted back. Then he turned and spoke to Lightfoot.

"Four horses!" he said succinctly.

"Two!" offered Johnny, suddenly flashing up two fingers. And the whole crowd joined in on the haggling. Hands went up and fingers were raised—some clamoring for four, some for three—and Horse-Ketchum unlashed a pack. From its kyack he lifted out a big sack of flour, a can of coffee, a bag of sugar and two plugs of trade tobacco. He laid them on the ground and pointed to his man, then held up two fingers again.

Once more in a clamor of shouting the clansmen argued and gesticulated, but Panamint Tom stood unmoved. He was their chief and he withheld his voice.

"Here!" spoke up Johnny, offering a sack of tobacco and a block of matches for *pilon*; and the chief of the Shoshones unbent. He rolled a cigarette, while Lightfoot rolled another and passed a sack of makings through the crowd. Then as the smoke drifted up and Horse-Ketchum flashed two fingers the people shouted acclaim. Panamint Tom nodded gravely, Eatum-up Jake accepted the presents—and Captain Jack rose up, ransomed.

CHAPTER XXII

THE DEATH-WATCH

A BIG feast was on in the camp of the Shoshones when a yell rose up from the lookout on the hill and Jim Chatfield came out to the gate. Since the quarrel over Captain Jack he had not spoken to Horse-Ketchum, who was camped out under the trees; but after a brief glance up the road he strode out towards him, and Johnny saw that his anger had passed.

"You'd better come inside the fence," he said. "That's Bodie again, on your trail."

"Much obliged," answered Lightfoot. "But I'm not scared of him a bit, so—"

"Well, bring your Injun with you," broke in Chatfield gruffly. And Captain Jack threw the packs on the mules. Up went the kyacks, and the lash-ropes were tied any way. Then horses and mules alike were rushed through the gateway, while Jack looked back and laughed. His life had been spared at the intercession of his master; but the Shoshones had bristled like angry dogs when he passed, and Eatum-up Jake had snarled balefully. But now, inside the gate, he was safe from them all; and Bodie had halted up the road.

"Reckon he's looking for High Behind," suggested Johnny exultantly. "Every time that whelp steals anything I steal it right back from him. He was digging around your wagons when I passed."

"Oh, he was, eh?" exclaimed Chatfield, and then he nodded grimly. "I know what's biting him," he said. "One of my Indians, when we were digging there, found a fine gold watch. They're trying to locate that treasure-box."

"He's afraid," jeered Lightfoot, stepping out into the open where Bodie and his men could see him. "He's on the dodge himself, and if those stampeders ever catch him they'll hang him for a certainty. So I suppose he's come down to lift my scalp."

"No, he's after mine," stated Chatfield. "Did you bring back those cartridges? Well, you saved my bacon that time, because there's Riley Sloper. And Riley is a clean-strain killer."

He pronounced the words calmly, almost as if they were words of praise; and Horse-Ketchum saw in the level glance of Chatfield's eyes that he too was a killer, and proud of it.

"No, Riley is after me," he continued imperson-ally. "He's Dad Tolliver's right-hand man, sent out to track me down. And according to the code he can't go back until he kills me, or I get him. But Mistuh Lightfoot, I hate to kill him—because Damaris, my wife, is a Tolliver. So I'm going to wait for the heat."

"Wait!" echoed Lightfoot. "My Lord, ain't this hot enough?"

"You wait till July," returned Chatfield, "and every fly on this ranch will drop dead. They gather under the leaves on the north side of the house and fall to the ground in windrows. That's heat—the kind that kills people. And I don't reckon Riley can stand it."

"Well, I can," asserted Johnny. "I've got to stay, Jim. Because, Bodie or no Bodie, I'm going back to get Diana."

"You won't leave this ranch for a month," pre-dicted Chatfield, as the Night Riders rode back up the road. "Those rascals have gone back to camp at Cow Springs—they'll be watching us, night and day."

"Let 'em watch," answered Horse-Ketchum, "I'll sneak off after dark. I reckon your Shooshonnies are going."

He pointed to the hilltop where the Indians in a compact body were watching the retreat of the Night Riders. But, despite their warlike front, the women along the ditch-bank were packing their

179

bundles to go. The great heat had come but, much as they feared it, they feared Val Bodie more. For, though he was married to a squaw, his kinsmen were Piutes, with whom the Shoshones were continually at war. And he had a ruthless way, with Indians, of shooting first and talking afterwards which had intimidated even Panamint Tom.

"Me stay!" spoke up Captain Jack at his elbow; and Chatfield looked him over appraisingly. With his scouts and retainers gone he would need the Indian's services, but he only glanced dourly at Lightfoot.

"All right, Jack," responded Johnny. "You stay inside this fence and Eatum-up Jake won't get you. I'll take care of you, savvy? Any time!"

"By grab!" laughed Chatfield, "you shore think a lot of that Injun, standing up against that bunch the way you did. I don't trust 'em very far, myself."

"Me good Injun!" stated Jack. "Horse-Ketchum good Hiko man. We friends, eh?" And he held out his hand.

"You bet ye!" returned Johnny, shaking hands with him indulgently. "And we'll stick together, Jack. Then bymeby, when it gets hot, if you help me steal my woman I'll let you go back to your wife."

"Ho! Good!" assented Jack, striding off to unpack the mules; and the white men sought the shelter of the house.

Already in the south a solid wall of dust

announced the approach of another sandstorm. The trees were whipping in the wind; and about them, finer than sand, the storm-borne silt was dropping. It touched their sweaty hands and set in tiny cakes that formed grey spots of cement; and all the time as the wind howled louder the size of the gravel grew. But behind their stout stockade they escaped its full force, and the corridor between the houses was cool.

All that night, watch and watch, the two white men stood guard; but Val Bodie and his men did not come. Horse-Ketchum rose at dawn and looked out over a sand-strewn world, so desolate and empty that they seemed like human atoms, set down in a bottomless void. Yet up on the sharp-topped butte where the Shoshones had kept their watch a man sat, sphinx-like, his gun across his knees, his back humped against the wind.

"It's Riley Sloper!" pronounced Chatfield. "The death-watch is set. But I don't want to kill him. He's a Tolliver."

"Well, maybe," hinted Lightfoot, "I can take him off your hands. You know what I said—to Little Jim."

"Little Jim is a Tolliver, too," responded his father slowly. "No, Johnny, let's wait for the heat."

The blazing sun topped the Funeral Range and no wind came sweeping in, to mitigate its sullen intensity. By ten in the morning, the salt marshes had begun to steam, and the death-watch left his butte. A black haze rose up from the miles of slimy sink, where the poisonous brine stewed and smoked; and there came to their nostrils the rank odor of that hell's brew which had snuffed out so many lives.

The cattle gathered along the ditches, half-immersed in the running water; the chickens sneaked into the house; and there, before the fan, dogs and humans alike stretched out to endure the heat. It came up from the marshes in panting waves, like the breath of some monster of the deep; as if the crater which once yawned there had opened its vents again, giving off its poison vapors in gasps. All the world seemed a furnace, an oven where men were baked, and Little Jim fretted and wailed.

"Poor little boy!" sighed his mother again and again as she held him before the whirling wheel; and as the cool water splashed over him a wry smile twisted his face, which was mottled with the blistering heat. The hot weather had come, and a huge hand seemed to cover them, crushing them down with malignant hate. As the men paced about, keeping watch for their enemies, they wore towels about their necks to wipe off the blinding sweat which ran down into their eyes. Yet when the sun, like a ball of fire, set behind the towering Panamints, a gaunt form again showed itself on the butte. It was Riley Sloper, and in the madness of the heat Jim Chatfield reached for his gun.

"No!" he cursed, as his wife clutched his hand. "It's him or me—that's the code."

"Oh, but wait, Jim, wait!" she pleaded. "Think of Little Jim—and me. Don't shoot—God will strike him with His heat."

"But it's hell," complained Chatfield, "in the bottom of this sink. God never intended a white man to live here. If I kill him we can go up on the peaks!"

He waved one hand petulantly towards the high summits of the Panamints, where the pine-trees stood out against the sky. But she dissuaded him from his purpose and as the night came on they chained the high door of the gate. In the blank darkness of the desert night Jim took up his weary march, ready to fight in defense of his life; but each morning with the dawn the haunting figure came back, to look down from the top of the butte.

"I'll kill him!" swore Chatfield; but each time he held his hand and God sent a greater heat. Puffy clouds rose up like burnished cones of fire and hung motionless above the high peaks. They rode up against the wind and turned black at the base. Then a long spout reached down and the cloud-burst broke with a thunder that shattered the air. The water poured out in long black feelers that spread to a solid column. It rained, and down some canyon a wall of brushwood came, spewed out by the glut behind. Then trees and yellow water, and boulders that ground and tumbled, until they rolled far out on the flat. The flood spent its force with magical quickness and as the last rush cleared the canyon its front swept down into the sink.

Before a pageantry like this they lived on day by day as the rainy season reached its height; but not a drop came to cool their fevered lips, for the bottom of the valley was dry. Nor did the thirsty mountains feel the wash of driving rains. Some canyon, parched before, was inundated by a flood—the rest of the desert remained dry. It was a scene to make men ponder on the majesty of God; but the fever in their brains, the smiting heat that burned their eyeballs, made them curse His very Name. They endured, since they must, and every day at dawn Riley Sloper stood out on his butte.

Never once in a month of waiting had he ventured near the ranch, though they knew what his errand was. He seemed in his crack-brained way to be courting the very death which Dad Tolliver had sent him to deal. An ambush at dawn, a bullet from the brush as he stepped out against the sky, and this clean-strain killer of the Tolliver clan would be wiped out by a shot. Yet, crazed as Chatfield was, his wife over-persuaded him and the watch of death went on. But Val Bodie and his men had long since left, and one evening Horse-Ketchum saddled Paynim.

By the banks of the rushing ditch, tied as it were to a hay-stack, the golden stallion had fretted impatiently—and always he looked to the north. Now as he felt his master's hand and champed the familiar bit he snuffed the heated wind and whickered. He knew without words that their ride would take him home, to the canyon where his mates frisked and played.

"Be quiet!" admonished Lightfoot, laying a hand on his nose as he passed him out the tall gate; and Paynim snorted softly. Then as Horse-Ketchum swung up he ambled off through the night until at last he broke into a lope. Cow Springs lay behind them, his feet were in the trail, and ahead were Moonbeam—and Diana.

CHAPTER XXIII

THE HAND OF GOD

A BLANKET of clouds overhung Devil Mountain as Horse-Ketchum rode north through the night; and above Enúpi Gai the heat-lightning stabbed and blinked, brewing a storm for the coming day. Strange winds came rushing in, whipping the sand-hills to a spume, which leapt up against the murky sky; but Paynim kept on, ever tugging at the bit, never tiring, though the heat brought the sweat. And as he loped on he whickered, softly.

All his life had been spent in this valley of death, where only the strongest could survive. He was desert-bred, and his sires before him had known nothing but sand and heat. Horse-Ketchum dropped the reins and gave him his head, but on the shore of the dry lake Paynim stopped. There was a shimmer in the star-light—water lapped at his feet. The dry lake had come back to its own, and the clouds above the peaks rumbled bodingly.

The stallion turned away, fighting his head to circle the lake, trotting anxiously until he found the familiar wash; but at the entrance to the gateway, where the rock dam blocked their path, he snorted and came to a halt. Then he neighed, loud and shrill, his heart wild with longing. But no mate answered his call. He neighed louder, in frenzied appeal, dropping his nose to the ground in a long, sobbing grunt of despair. Now at last he knew the reason why his master had not turned homeward and he turned back towards Toógahboth with a sigh.

The dawn found them safely hidden among the ancient mesquites, whose roots, while their tops were bathed in fire, drank deep of the flood water at their feet. There was no water-hole now, to tempt the wild mustangs to their fate. All the broad, silvery flat where the moon-horses had gamboled was covered by an inch-deep sea. Every day some barren canyon belched out its charge of waters to fill up the shallow lake, but quick as it came the sun drank it up, while the clouds poured down more rain.

As the sun swung up, like a flaming shield before the face of an angry God, Horse-Ketchum saw the thunderheads rise, higher and higher above the mountains until they puffed out in fluffy white cones. They turned black at the base and between two monstrous clouds the lightning stabbed back and forth, threateningly. Then they moved together, slowly, while the canyons re-echoed to the rumble of their thunderous booming. The mighty forces of nature seemed set in battle array, cloud bearing down on cloud while the storm-gods who rode their crests smote the earth with their bolts of fire.

Beneath them, stunned and awed by the majesty of the combat, Horse-Ketchum watched the cohorts of the sky as they wheeled above the mountain peaks. What if, among those canyons, the gods should descend upon Diana's and scour out the dam at its gateway! With what joy, like a Prince Charming, he would ride up the new-made road and bring her the news of her freedom! But the clouds swung away, further and further to the north, retiring sullenly with muttered detonations.

A sense of loss and disappointment, of thwarted hope and unreasoning fear, drove Lightfoot to the shelter of the trees. How could he, a mere atom in the cosmos, hope to turn the forces of nature to do his will? And yet he watched, for a man can hope. Every day the storm struck somewhere—some canyon was swept bare. And how could Devil

Canyon escape, when others on both sides had caught the sluicing descent of the cloudbursts? There was a crash along the peaks, a thunderous reverberation which announced that the storm-gods had struck, and as Horse-Ketchum leapt up he felt the earth tremble beneath him, with the shock of another, mightier stroke. Then with a smashing clap of thunder the two clouds rushed together and their base turned black as ink.

The bottom broke and a snaky water-spout reached down towards the jagged peaks, whipping back and forth—seeking the spot. Where it fell the waste of ages would be swept clean away, leaving the bed-rock white and bare. Johnny found himself praying, trying to move with his puny hands this avalanche of water across the sky. But it drifted off to the north and as the solid column fell he could see that Devil Canyon had escaped.

The cloud opened, like a bag from which the bottom is ripped, and the rain poured, inky-black, through the hole. As if drawn in by the suction the thunderhead floated above it, sagging lower till the peaks were obscured. Lightfoot waited expectantly, his eyes on the canyons to the north; until at last a leaping mass belched out of its narrow throat and swept down towards the lake. Another followed, and he saw the impetuous rush of the torrent as it battled its way out through the passage. Then from Devil Canyon itself a mountain of rocks shot forth, with a roar that stopped his heart.

The spout had shifted, behind its curtain of mist, touching the head-waters of three canyons as it fell; and the barrier across the gateway had gone down. A deluge of yellow foam overleaped it and swept on, carrying tree-trunks on its crest like straws; and through his glasses Lightfoot could see the churning waves of the torrent as they bore the shattered boulders along. There was no room before its front for anything that could move and it swept the gateway clean with a rush. The forefront of the water moved forward like a wall, spreading out as the sand-washes diverted it, and before the first wave had lapped into the turbid lake the glut at the gateway had passed. The resistless hand of Nature had performed within an hour the work of a thousand men.

Horse-Ketchum was astounded by the swiftness of this Hand which had opened the way before him. He felt as if in some way he had broken the dam himself, by the force of his muttered prayer. He felt great, exalted, the particular god of all that land where nobody dwelt but him. But as the waters spent their strength and the washes ran quickly dry he shook off the spell which had held him in its thrall and threw the saddle on Paynim.

Devil Canyon was open and he circled the muddy lake till he stood on the bank of the wash. The level sand was firm—it had set like cement—and Paynim stepped out on it confidently. Then, fighting his head, he trotted off up the wash until he stood before the shattered gateway. The great wall which had towered there had been swept clean away, filling up the deep pool of the waterfall. Their way had been made straight by the hand of God Himself, and Paynim raised his head and neighed.

Up over the battered wall he scrambled on the jump, splashing madly through the water as they forded the muddy creek, which was running knee-deep among the rocks. All about them lay the wreckage of the trees and fields above, the stranded trunks of cottonwoods, scattered remnants of the fence, an orepan from Morgan's mine. Horse-Ketchum had a vision of the canyon as it had been before the cloudburst had worked its will. The same Hand which had opened the gateway might have destroyed all behind it—the golden horses, the mine, Diana! But who could doubt a God who had given so much? He pressed on, and the cave appeared before him.

The wave of mud from the first rush of the flood had been halted almost at its door, where the cowhide still hung by its thongs, and the trees along the canyon wall stood firm. But down the middle of the creek-bed a huge trench had been sluiced—trees, garden, fence and all, were gone. The surging waters had overwhelmed them, half burying them in débris, and then the run-off had cut a deep ditch. Johnny reined over towards the cave, overcome by gloomy thoughts, starting nervously at every sound.

The canyon was empty now and only the babbling creek woke the echoes of the pent-house walls. But on the cliff, not a month before, he had seen a golden head—and Diana's fox, making off. He had seen her father, too, waving his rifle like a madman as he poised on the edge of the abyss. What if he was lurking now, waiting to wreak a belated revenge? What if Diana has been lost in the flood? He halted before the doorway, too unstrung to venture in, and as they listened Paynim pricked up his ears. Then he whirled and raised his head and, loud and shrill against the wind, he gave the call to his mates.

There was a silence, while the water babbled louder over its rocks and the cliffs echoed back the neigh; but Paynim had heard what his master could not hear and he started at a trot up the creek. Johnny saw a track before him, sunk deep in the half-dried mud, the imprint of huge moccasins, leading the way in long strides—the footprints of Frying-pan George. Yet he did not draw rein for, across the ravaged creek-bed, the wooded pasture lay unspoiled. Tossing heads rose and fell among the clustering mesquite trees, where a herd of horses came running. Then, out from the thorny thicket, Diana came at a gallop, and behind her the nine golden steeds.

She stopped short at sight of Paynim—and a strange man in her canyon where before only her father had dwelt—but when Johnny raised his hand she swung low on Moonbeam's neck and came plunging up the cut-bank of the creek. Her hair was flying wildly, she was splashed with sand and mud, but her eyes glowed like stars when she met him face to face and dropped down, trembling, from her horse.

"Oh, Johnny!" she cried, throwing her arms about his neck. "I'm so *glad!*" And she gave him a hug. "Oh—Johnny!" she breathed again and kissed him on both cheeks. "I never looked to see you again!"

"Here too!" responded Horse-Ketchum, returning the hug and kisses gaily. "I was down there at Night Water when the cloudburst opened the gateway. And believe me, I rode right up!"

"Up the canyon? Is it open? Oh, then Johnny, we must run. Because if Father comes back he'll kill you."

"I reckon he will," assented Lightfoot. "Let's be riding, right now. There's his tracks, going up to the mine."

"He's crazy!" she whispered. "The storm washed off half his ore, that he'd piled up by the dump. I was afraid to go near him, he cursed and shouted so. Oh, Johnny, I'm glad you've come!"

She buried her face against his breast and he patted her soothingly while his eyes searched the country above. The cloudburst had come down the narrow canyon to the north, where Morgan had driven his tunnel. Then, taking a sharp turn, it had piled up a mountain of débris and swept on down the creek. Rocks and boulders were strewn everywhere, cemented fast in mud, and somewhere in that chaos Randolph Morgan was searching for his gold.

"Let's go—right now!" spoke up Johnny. And he kissed her as he turned to mount.

She was pale and frightened now, and yet her eyes as she looked back at him were big and tender with love.

"Yes—Johnny," she answered, and scrambled up on Moonbeam, who was standing nose to nose with Paynim. Then with a kick of the heel she dashed ahead toward the cave, dropping off to dart in through the door.

Horse-Ketchum followed fast, one eye on the trail behind, the other on the cowhide door.

"Come on!" he called. "Don't stop for your clothes. My God, don't take so long!"

A frenzy of impatience came over him as he waited, but Diana lingered on.

"I'm getting Mother's jewels," she replied in muffled tones. "But he seems to have hidden them, somewhere."

"Let 'em go!" he yelled. "Do you want me to get killed?" And from far up the canyon there came a shout.

"Come out of that!" he cried, dropping down off his horse to rush inside the door.

"I've found them!" she responded, running out

of an inner chamber. "But Johnny, I can't find Christopher!"

"Christopher who?" he demanded, catching her up in his arms and carrying her out the door. "Can't you hear? Your father is coming!"

"Yes, but Christopher!" she sobbed. "My dear little fox, you know! And oh, now Columbus is gone!"

"Let 'em go," entreated Lightfoot, "and pile up on that horse!" And as he spoke a savage shouting rent the air. It was Morgan, cursing the storm as he strode back from his mine. But he had not rounded the turn. Horse-Ketchum caught the glint of a rifle in his hands as he came around the point, and snatched Diana in a panic.

"Ride," he yelled, "or I'll be killed, sure as hell!" And he swung her up on her horse. Paynim reared and flew back, but he mounted on the fly and they were off in a shower of mud. Hanging low on Paynim's neck Lightfoot listened for the bullets, but the old man did not shoot. He was running like a madman to catch a horse from the *remuda*. But as he ran he held fast to his gun.

"He's coming!" warned Johnny, and took the lead like a shot. It was Paynim, the sire, against his son—the stallion against his own flesh and blood—and to lose the race meant death.

CHAPTER XXIV

THE GREAT HEAT

THE sun gleamed like fire on the flooded floor of the dry lake as Horse-Ketchum raced out of Devil Canyon, and the steam of drying mud along the course of the cloudburst made Lost Valley smoke like a cauldron. No wind stirred the sultry air, and even while they rode Lightfoot felt the blinding stroke of the heat. Yet the devil-man was behind them and, though death lay ahead, he spurred on into the abyss.

Around the shore of the shallow lagoon they rode side by side, Diana still clutching the casket of jewels which had tempted her to dally too long. Now she knew that, for her heirlooms, she might lose her lover, or compel him to kill her father. Yet even as she fled, looking back up the long wash, she remembered her precious pet foxes. It was for them more than the jewels that she had searched the darkened cave, and she murmured their names regretfully.

"Never mind about Christopher!" answered Horse-Ketchum shortly. "We've got to ride these horses down to get away from your father. They can't go far in this heat."

"Oh, there he comes, now!" cried Diana. "On Turco!"

A flash of gold at the canyon mouth turned to a thoroughbred racer, driven on at a furious pace by the old man on his back, who waved his rifle as he spied them. Johnny had circled the lake but Morgan charged into it impetuously, cutting across on a tangent to bring him within rifle-shot, recking nothing of the perils ahead. Almost before they knew it he had made up half the distance; but in the middle of the lake, where the bottom was soft, Turco labored and almost stopped.

"Come on!" yelled Lightfoot as Diana looked back fearfully. "He's stuck—he'll have to turn back! Let him shoot if he wants to—we'll keep up ahead of him and lose him in the sand-hills tonight!"

Morgan urged his racer on, deeper and deeper into the slough, but the more Turco floundered the more he became bogged until at last he came to a halt. The madman on his back had driven him so far, but Turco knew the mud-holes ahead. Since he had been a colt he had waded in the lake, when the cloudbursts flooded the playa with mud; but where the water had stood longest no horse or man could cross and he turned stubbornly back towards the shore. Morgan fought him in a fury and, when they won the further shore, Horse-Ketchum and Diana were gone.

Down the Death Valley trail, past the ever-drifting sand-hills which radiated a suffocating heat, they fled on regardless of the precious animals they rode—horses worth almost their weight in gold. The blood of kings coursed in their veins, but now they felt the whip; and so they galloped till the night closed down. They had escaped, though behind them Morgan was spurring on their trail; for the darkness would hide them, now.

Lightfoot turned out of the burro-path which led on to Esahbwoó, where the emigrants had perished long before, and dismounted to breathe his mount. And noble-hearted Paynim, his shoulders flecked with foam, spread his forefeet and blowed like a grampus. The race had sapped his strength, after the long ride the night before and his day in the sweltering heat; but after his master had rubbed him down and patted his neck he turned and followed Moonbeam south. He had won her again, the queen of his *manada*; but a heat had come upon them that almost stopped their breath and he took the trail at a walk.

Never before in his long stay at Furnace Creek had Horse-Ketchum known such a night. Even after the sun had set the ground gave off heat, as if the crater far beneath them had come to life. The earth seemed to sweat out a poisonous gas—the rank smell of decaying marshes, cooking and stewing like a hellbroth—and the air moved in hot, blasting gasps. After daring storm and flood to rescue Diana from her canyon he had brought her into the stark presence of death.

Always before as the night wore on the air had

become cooler, but now the heat seemed to increase. To save their spent horses they dismounted and walked, stopping often to listen for pursuit; and in the silence of the desert Johnny told her of her cousins, and of the welcome which awaited them at the ranch. It appeared before them at dawn, like a mirage in the distance, and Paynim pricked up his ears. The tall palms brought up visions of running water and shady nooks, and Moonbeam whickered joyously.

"Another mile and we're there," said Lightfoot, mounting; and Diana swung in beside him. Her face was pale and bloodless from the exhaustion that comes from heat, but as they trotted towards the ranch she smiled.

"Isn't it beautiful!" she sighed. "Is that Cousin Jim at the gate? But who is that other man? He's running!"

She pointed to the butte down which a scarecrow figure was coming, and Horse-Ketchum jumped Paynim into a gallop.

"Come on!" he yelled. "That's Riley Sloper— he's a Tolliver! Been trying to kill Jim for a month!"

He looked back towards the butte, where day after day the feudist had kept his death-watch; but now Sloper was shambling towards him at a crazy, high-stepping lope.

"He's locoed with the heat!" cried Lightfoot in dismay, as Riley stopped and whipped up his gun.

And as if they sensed their danger the two horses raced away, while their riders swung low along their necks. Sloper had halted on a knoll, his neck craned, his rifle extended as he followed the course of their race; but as he drew a bead on Johnny there was a shot from the gate and he jumped and dropped his gun. Jim Chatfield had been watching him and now, after months of jockeying, the rival clansmen were shooting it out.

Sloper ducked behind a bush and made a run to get his gun; but with the sureness of death itself, Chatfield's rifle spoke again and his enemy went down, sprawling. A puff of dust had risen before him, there was a commotion behind the brush; and then, left-handed, Riley Sloper drew his pistol and shot back at the man he aimed to kill. But when, deliberately, Jim raised his rifle to shoot, he ran like a wounded buck.

"I winged him!" shouted Chatfield as Lightfoot rode up to the gate. "Take her in to Damaris—he'll be back."

He stepped aside to let them pass, his keen eyes following Sloper's flight, and that was Diana's welcome to Furnace Creek.

But once inside the gateway Damaris came running and greeted her with a kiss.

"Are you Diana?" she cried. "Diana Morgan? Then come right in, dear, out of the heat!"

Johnny gazed after them dumbly as they passed in, arm and arm, to seek the cool darkness of the house; and as Captain Jack hurried out to take charge of the horses he staggered in and wet his throbbing head. Though the sun had hardly risen it was like the heat of midday and he stretched out with a sigh before the fan. Without the splash of its water, the busy swirl of its sturdy wings, how else could a man hope to endure the day to come, and the inferno of another night? He closed his blood-shot eyes and breathed deep as his muscles relaxed—then he passed into a dreamless sleep.

For two nights and a day, without sleep, or rest, he had ridden on his quest; and now, safely home, he left Diana to her kinfolks, and Jim to guard the gate. The crack of a rifle roused him and Captain Jack rushed in, seeking shelter from the fray.

"Devil-man—she come!" he gasped, rolling his eyes. "Devil-man, from Enúpi Gai! Riley Sloper run shoot him—Jim Chatfield shootum. Fightum now—devil-man fall down."

"Hell's bells!" exclaimed Horse-Ketchum as he looked about for his guns, "the old man is on the war-path!" But when he ran out to the gate Randolph Morgan was on the ground and his horse was standing over him.

"They've gone crazy, both of them!" cursed Chatfield, his eyes gleaming wickedly. "Riley Sloper went hog wild and came down to kill him and the old man rode out to meet him. They were shooting it out when I ran Riley off. Do you reckon that's my uncle Randolph?"

"I know it," answered Lightfoot. "And he was crazy before he started. Came down here on purpose to kill me, so I'm glad he tangled with Riley. By grab, Jim, this is getting dangerous!"

"Well, let's go out and bring him in," responded Chatfield shortly, "before he perishes in the sun. And then Riley Sloper can play hell, if he wants to. I'm going to get back to that fan."

He started down the road, still watching the brush for the hob-goblin form of Sloper; but the feudist had fled up the bank of the ditch and they hurried on to Morgan.

He lay piled up among the rocks just as his horse in flying back had dumped him on his head, one outstretched hand still clutching the pistol with which he had been firing when he fell. Lightfoot looked him over grimly as he kicked aside the hot gun and helped lay him across the back of his horse. Except for the accident of his chance encounter with Riley Sloper the old man's gun would have been turned on him. But now he was stunned by his fall among the boulders and they bore him back to the house.

"He's crazy—we're all crazy!" croaked Chatfield as they laid Morgan in front of the fan. "The man don't live that can stand out in that sun and not have his brains begin to cook. For cripes' sake, take care of him while I soak my haid!" And he plunged his head into the ditch.

Johnny followed him, for the exertion in the

broiling sun had made his senses reel. He was dizzy, and the throb of blood in his brain was like a hammer-stroke against his skull. The world seemed obscured and as he lay gasping before the fan he dreamt crazily of fighting and sudden death. Riley Sloper—Randolph Morgan—they met and merged before his eyes into a creature of inconceivable hate; and then the saturnine visage of Jim Chatfield appeared, his keen eyes gleaming murderously. They were all out to kill—the heat had overthrown their reason. But the fan was bringing it back.

Lightfoot felt the splash of water against his face—warm water, almost hot, but turning cool in an instant before the breeze stirred up by the fan. How had anyone lived in that inferno of heat before the fan had been set in place? The same water that turned the mill-wheel splashed the ground and the people on it, people who sprawled on the wet earth as abject as animals, asking nothing but to drink, and drink again. In that furnace-like atmosphere a pint of water was nothing. They drank gallons of it in a day and from every pore at once the blinding sweat poured out.

He glanced up at the women who sat close to the fan, with little Jim lying between them, stark naked on a piece of wet cloth. His face was as mottled as a new-born babe's but his little body was cool. Randolph Morgan lay next, his white beard whipping in the breeze, his eyes closed as if in death. But his breast rose rhythmically and Johnny knew he was alive. And, with him, to be alive was to be dangerous. Jim Chatfield sat close to Lightfoot, his back against the wall, his lantern jaws grimly set. He alone watched the gateway, and at his side lay the rifle which had sent so many Tollivers to their reward.

Horse-Ketchum dozed off, wondering vaguely at the fate which had led him to such a place. Not a day's journey away the Shoshones were looking down on them from high mountains, covered with pines. But they, the superior white people, lay frying in their fat to feed some ancient grudge. It was the feud which had driven them every one to this inferno—Jim Chatfield, Riley Sloper, Randolph Morgan. And what a breed of fighters they were! So dangerous and yet so loyal, willing to lay down their lives for their clan! Even the heat had not driven them to a truce.

Behind them all, his stolid face beaded with sweat, sat the Indian, Captain Jack. He was stripped to the waist, his sturdy feet were bare, and at sight of his master he grinned. This valley was his home, the ancient dwelling-place of his people, and patiently he endured the torment. But as he sat there he too watched the gate. Somewhere out in the hills, wounded and crazed by the heat, Riley Sloper roamed at large, as dangerous as a side-winder, ready to strike at the first thing that moved.

A black haze, like a pall of smoke, obscured the

sun as the marshes boiled, filling the air with a sweltering humidity; and in a darkness like that of an eclipse the sufferers fell silent, as if the end of the world were at hand. Such a heat as they endured had never been felt before—the thermometer stood at a hundred and thirty-four—and men, dogs and chickens, even the woodrats from the mesquite-pile, laid themselves out in the track of the fan. But suddenly, when the fever in their blood was at its highest, the splashing of the water-wheel ceased.

Jim Chatfield rose up, muttering fretfully under his breath as he hurried to look at the flume. Then his voice rang out sharply in a staccato of angry curses, and Damaris started up anxiously.

"What's the matter, dear?" she called, and his answer was like a death sentence.

"The ditch is dry!" he yelled. "Riley Sloper has cut it. Ketch some water or we won't have a drop!"

CHAPTER XXV

UP THE DITCH

THERE is a madness which comes from heat, making the wanderer on the desert run in circles and dig holes in the sand. It drives prospectors to kill their partners for a canteen of water, and the only escape is to rest. Lying still in the shade, though the blood pounds like mad and the senses reel from the sun, the slender thread of reason holds men back from a race to their death. But once they begin to run they are lost.

Before the cool draft of their fan the heat-sick people at Furnace Creek had escaped the ultimate madness that brings death, but with the water-wheel stilled they leapt up one by one in a fever of distracted fear. Damaris clutched her baby, trying to still its feeble wails. Jim Chatfield reached for his gun. But when he started up the ditch, muttering threats against Riley Sloper, his wife caught him by the arm.

"Jim," she said, "if you go it will kill you. No man can live in that sun."

"Riley Sloper lived!" he yapped. "He lived to cut my ditch. I believe he waited on purpose."

"No, now Jim, dear," she reasoned, "Riley is out of his head. We can stand it until night, and then you can go up there. But if you go now, it will mean your death."

"I'm going to kill Riley Sloper if it's my last act!" raved Chatfield. "This is murder—killing women and children! And who's going to mend the ditch, unless I do it?" he demanded.

"I will!" spoke up Horse-Ketchum. But as he reached for a shovel Captain Jack pushed him gently aside.

"Me go!" he said. "You lay down—keep still. Pretty soon you hear water come back."

"All right, Jack," smiled Johnny. "I believe you

can stand it. But if one of us Hiko men goes out in that sun—"

"No good—killum dead!" nodded the Indian. And with an answering smile he was gone.

They lay down in the sweltering corridor, where the hot dampness from the wet ground seemed almost to stop their breath, and so the long ordeal began. But one by one they rose up and went outside, for their veins seemed running with fire. There was no water left to drink, and a hot wind from the sink made their lips dry up and crack. The leaves on the lush cottonwoods hung curled up and drooping; and as the swallows from under the leaves felt the mad urge to fly they dropped dead as they circled the fields. The world was burning up, and they were burning with it, without even the chance of a drink.

In tense silence or cursing brokenly Jim Chatfield paced the porch, looking off up the ditch for Captain Jack. But the Indian had disappeared, creeping slowly up the stream-bed to gain the scant shade of the mesquites.

"I'm going!" repeated Chatfield, over and over like a litany. But Damaris shook her head. Little Jim had begun to wail, with thin, choking cries that stabbed at his mother's heart; but she sat beside him, fanning, while Diana on the other side put the last drop of water to his lips. Horse-Ketchum had waited, but now as he met her eyes he beckoned Jim Chatfield aside.

"You stay here," he said. "I'm going up the ditch." And Chatfield nodded glumly.

"All right," he answered. "Damn an Injun anyway. Much obliged, Johnny—it's my turn next."

He turned and paced away, but as Lightfoot started up the ditch he heard the gurgle of water at his feet. It came rushing, as if eager to run down the flume and dash against the paddles of the wheel, and Horse-Ketchum whooped as it passed.

"Here it comes!" he yelled. "Here's the water! Water!" And the great wheel groaned on its gudgeons. Then with a splash from its paddles it sent the broad wings spinning and everyone came running. They were laughing like children as they drank deep and wet their heads and laid the baby out on damp sacks; but as they settled down to rest Lightfoot remembered his Indian, for Captain Jack had not come back.

"Oh, he's all right," reasoned Jim. "They's no use going up there. I'd just have to go out after you." And so they waited until the sun sank behind the Panamints and the terrible day was done.

But when evening approached and Captain Jack did not come, Horse-Ketchum started off up the ditch.

"Wait a minute," called Chatfield, "and I'll go along with you. He may have had trouble with Riley."

He wrapped a rag around his rifle and hung it

through his arm, for the metal was blistering hot, and as they moved up towards the hills Johnny saw his keen eyes searching out every tree and bush.

"If I find that Riley Sloper," he said at last, "I'll shoot him like a dog. A man is a fool to listen to his womenfolks—I should have killed him, long ago."

"I believe you're right," nodded Horse-Ketchum. "I couldn't savvy what he was waiting for—"

"The murdering whelp was waiting to kill my wife—and my baby, that's half a Tolliver! But he knowed his only chance—and not get hung for it—was to ketch us in a big spell of heat. A man like that don't deserve no pity. I'll kill him like a broken-back rattlesnake!"

Chatfield strode ahead, muttering, but as he approached the mouth of the canyon Captain Jack rose up and pointed. Then he held up a rifle and a pair of six-shooters and the white men understood. Crawling and groveling down a dry wash, his clothes torn from his back and his matted hair covering his face, Riley Sloper, stark mad, was whimpering like a fox as he dug furtive holes in the sand. Jim Chatfield watched him coldly, then glanced at the break where Captain Jack had mended the ditch.

"Did he do that?" he asked. And Jack nodded.

"She crazy," he grinned. "All time diggum hole. All time cry—say killum little boy."

"Yes, damn his cowardly heart!" gritted

Chatfield. "I knowed he done it on purpose. Cut that ditch, by grab, jest like he'd cut a man's throat. He knowed it would kill my boy."

He raised his rifle slowly, then dropped it to his side and slouched off down the gulch.

Riley Sloper was digging away against the cutbank of the wash, and when they came he did not stop or look up. His right hand was torn and bloody, where Chatfield's bullet had shattered it, his naked back was burned by the sun; but he dug on, talking to himself.

"Pore leetle feller—and a Tolliver, too. But Dad told me I had to kill Jim. He's a Chatfield, damn his heart, and he went and stole Damaris. Stole a Tolliver—and crossed the blood."

"Well, what of it, you danged skunk?" demanded Chatfield roughly, giving him a jab in the ribs with his gun. "Look up here and quit your diggin'—and say your prayers, if you know any—because I'm going to blow your haid off!"

Sloper fell over sidewise and stared up with vacant eyes, then turned to his ceaseless digging.

"Water!" he croaked. "I've got to find water. My Gawd, that sun is killing me. But I cain't go away—I've got to kill Jim first. He's a Chatfield and he done stole Damaris."

"He's crazy!" pronounced Chatfield. "Take him and throw him in the ditch. By God, I hate to shoot him. But you heard what he said—I've got my wife and baby to think of."

"Let's take him down to the house," proposed Lightfoot, as they watched Sloper drink at the ditch. "He was crazy when I came, at sun-up this morning. And what will the womenfolks say?"

"Yes, that's it," grumbled Jim. "I should've shot him on sight. Now Damaris will know—and of course he's a Tolliver. Well, tote him along, then—he's ganted down to a shadder. But they's no good will come from it. He's a killer."

They bore him back down the ditch, the mere skeleton of a man, and laid him down in front of the fan; and after Damaris had gazed fearfully at his stern and wasted countenance she turned and smiled up at her husband.

"I knew you wouldn't kill him," she said. "Oh, Jim!" And she kissed his cheek.

CHAPTER XXVI

THE FEUD

THE terrible night came on and they lay sprawling in front of the fan but towards midnight a great roaring aroused them, and the angry whoop of the wind. Then a sandstorm swept in, blowing away the humid vapors that had risen from the marshy sink, and one by one the sufferers slept. In front of the fan Little Jim's chubby fists relaxed and his feeble wail died away. His mother stretched out beside him—and tired and frightened Diana, who had fled in vain from her fate.

Now her father, tossing and muttering, lay side by side with Riley Sloper and both talked of killing as they slept. The old man, bent with years, and the stern and hardy feudist, and as she listened Diana wept. Her father had told the truth—all men were beasts and murderers. Even Johnny avoided her now. And the world she had dreamt of, behind the walls of her canyon—was this the land of her dreams? What heat, what madness, what tragedy lay all about her! And on the morrow—what would happen then? She crept closer to Damaris and put one hand in hers, and so she fell asleep.

Outside, the rush and rattle of the windstorm had ceased, and a coolness drew down into the Valley of Death that soothed the weary sleepers by the fan. Chatfield rose with the dawn and stood gazing at Riley Sloper, and the old man who huddled by his side. Then he took all the guns except his and Horse-Ketchum's and locked them up in his room. Death had come close enough during the madness of the heat. He beckoned, and Lightfoot followed him out.

"Watch Riley," he warned. "I'll take care of Uncle Randolph. I don't reckon he'll kill you, now."

"He thinks I stole his daughter," explained Johnny. "You tell him I brought her straight to you."

"I see," nodded Chatfield. "Well, I happen to

know you, Johnny; and I'll tell him you're a damned good man. A good man—and I'll never forget your starting off up that ditch. Let's go out and look after the stock."

They paced out wearily, like men old before their time, and on the bare ground before them they saw the bodies of swallows, struck dead as they flew through the heat. Under the fronds of the palms hawks and owls stared out, stupefied, still hiding from the long-vanished sun. But beneath the cottonwoods that stood along the ditch they found their horses, feeding. Paynim and Moonbeam looked up at Johnny and whickered—the heat had not even thinned their blood. But High Behind stood drooping, and at sight of his master he whinnied forth a frenzied appeal.

"He wants me to take him out of here," observed Horse-Ketchum grimly. "And I believe, by the gods, he's right."

"The heat's over," Chatfield assured him earnestly. "But we're lucky to come through alive. If it wasn't for Riley Sloper I'd leave here tomorrow. Stay around until we see which way he jumps."

"I'll stay," promised Johnny, "but you keep your eye on Morgan. I don't dare to speak to Diana."

"You'd better not," advised Jim, "until I get a chance to talk to him. But Riley is dangerous—he's a killer."

They threw down hay for their horses and started

a fire in the kitchen stove, and at the fragrance of boiling coffee all the sleepers arose, except Riley Sloper and Morgan. Sloper opened his eyes and stared up dully as he heard the women bustling about, but only when Damaris brought him a cup of hot coffee did he rouse up and look around.

"Where am I, ma'am?" he asked. "I seem to be sick—but I recollect seeing you, somewhar."

"You're with friends," she answered sweetly. "I'll take care of you, Mr. Sloper. Now take a good drink and you'll be stronger."

He clutched the cup feebly and drained it to the bottom and then he looked her over again.

"Why, you're Damaris!" he exclaimed. "I knowed I'd seen you somewhar. But what's the matter with my hand?"

He held up his bandaged arm and she saw his mind was wandering—he had forgotten where he was.

"You've been fighting!" she said reproachfully. "And somebody shot you. But Jim wrapped it and—"

"Jim?" he repeated. "Jim who?"

"Why, my husband!" she cried. "Didn't you know I was married? Jim Chatfield—and this is our baby."

She held up Little Jim, who had already been cared for, and the feudist regarded her strangely.

"I remember, now," he said. "I used to see him through my telescope—and you holding him, thar by the door. But did Jim Chatfield fix my hand?"

"Yes, and he went out and got you when you were crazy with the heat. You don't want to fight him—now, do you?"

"Not me!" answered Sloper. "I've got enough of fighting. And Jim Chatfield helped me—a Tolliver!"

"Yes, Riley, he helped you," she went on earnestly, "because Jim and I are married, now. He promised me he'd never fight the Tollivers again, except to protect his life."

"He hit me," spoke up Sloper, "but I don't reckon he meant to kill me. Because back home Jim was always a dead shot."

"He is now," said Damaris, "but Jim likes you, Riley. Won't you please shake hands and be friends?"

She bent over him pleadingly but his stern eyes flashed fire.

"I don't shake hands with no Chatfield!" he declared.

"Well, shake hands with Little Jim, then," she urged. "He's a Tolliver—James Tolliver Chatfield!" And she thrust out a tiny hand.

"I don't care if I do," stated Sloper judicially; and he took the little hand in his own. Then for a long time he sat staring at the mother and child and at last he beckoned her nearer.

"I'll shake hands with Jim," he said; and she ran to bring her husband.

"Jim," she beamed, "Riley has shook hands with Baby, and now he'll shake hands with you."

"No he won't!" burst out Chatfield as his anger got the better of him. And then he extended his hand. "All right, Riley," he said, "but damn your black heart, you tried to kill my wife and child!"

"I know it—I admit it," responded Sloper tremulously. "But Jim, I'm sorry I done it. Her own father told me to do it."

"My father!" she cried incredulously.

"Yes, ma'am, your own father, Dad Tolliver. But I reckon now he was out of his haid. He told me to find you, no matter whar you hid. It was a grievous thing to do, but I done it. But I don't reckon he knowed about Little Jim, hyar—and the blood being crossed, and all. The feud don't hold now—and I'm going to ask you, Jim, to take the hand of a Tolliver."

He held out his wounded hand, and as Chatfield took it grimly Damaris hugged her baby and wept.

CHAPTER XXVII

A BODIE MAN

THE feud which had cost its hundreds of lives—spreading down from the rugged mountains to the blue-grass valleys of Kentucky—was over, like the heat, in a day. Riley Sloper, who had gone through the tortures of hell to wreak vengeance for the insult to his clan, sat meekly in the shade while the man who had shot him applied balsam to his wounded hand. They said little, for old wounds are easily opened; but always while they worked Damaris hovered over them, and now her smile had returned.

She went about her tasks singing, as Horse-Ketchum had heard her when he sought refuge from Val Bodie and his gang; but now a greater enemy than Bodie was upon him, watching every move he made. Randolph Morgan was the last of the refugees to recover from the effects of the heat, but when he opened his eyes and saw Lightfoot talking with Chatfield he sat up and fixed him with his eyes.

"This is Johnny Lightfoot, Uncle," began Chatfield. "And I'm your nephew, Jim Chatfield."

"So you say," returned the old man, "but I don't know you at all, suh! That's the rascal who stole my daughter!"

He pointed a tremulous finger at Horse-Ketchum, and felt around for his gun.

"Where's my pistol?" he demanded. "Am I a prisoner in this house? Then give me back my guns!"

"You don't need no guns!" answered Chatfield shortly. "And before we go any further I'd like to correct you. Mistuh Lightfoot never stole your daughter."

"Yes he did!" accused Morgan. "And he stole my horse, too! He took Paynim—the best stallion in the band!"

"Paynim is out in the corral," spoke up Johnny. "He's yours, when you're ready to go."

"Yes, but where's my daughter, suh?" demanded the old man indignantly. "I saw you, you rascal! You took advantage of her innocence to deceive her and lead her astray! I saw you, suh, when you stole her—and all her mother's jewels—"

"Why, Father!" cried Diana, who had been listening at the doorway, "Johnny never even touched the jewels!"

"But he touched you!" raged Morgan. "I saw him, stealing your kisses. And what is more precious to a father's heart—his daughter's virtue or the jewels she wears?"

"Now, Uncle!" broke in Damaris, "I don't want you to talk that way. Because Diana asked Johnny to take her out of the canyon—and he brought her straight to us!"

"I don't know you, Madam," responded the old man tartly. "But I know my rights, and my duty as a father—"

"Then I'll inform you," answered Damaris, "that I'm Jim Chatfield's wife, and cousin by marriage to Diana. She's been placed in my care and no one, not even her father—"

"Let her speak for herself, then!" thundered Morgan, rising up and leaning shakily against the wall. "Diana, do you recognize my authority? Are you my daughter, or the cousin of this woman?"

"I'm your daughter," replied Diana meekly. "But Damaris is my cousin, too."

She slipped her hand into Damaris' and faced him fearlessly, while the old man's eyes bored her through.

"Answer my question!" he ordered. "Do you recognize my authority, or have you left my home?"

"I have left the canyon," answered Diana firmly. "Mother told me, when I grew up, that I should go—and take her jewels with me."

"Oh, she did, eh?" responded her father, after a silence. "Well, why didn't you say so, in the first place? It seems to me, after all my care, you might at least say good-by and not decamp like a runaway nigger!"

"Father!" cried Diana, "don't you speak to me like that! Don't you dare to call me such names! You don't love me any more—and now that Mother is gone I will stay here with Cousin Damaris."

"Very well!" bowed Morgan, taken aback by her anger. "I wash my hands of the whole matter. And now, if you will kindly bring up my horse I will leave this inhospitable roof."

He drew himself up proudly and turned to Jim, who advanced with a placating smile.

"No, no, Uncle Randolph," he protested, "we can't let you go like this. Come into the kitchen and Damaris will get your breakfast. You're too weak to go out in the heat."

"Well, I am weak," admitted the old man, as he tottered towards the door. "Something struck me—on the head."

"You fell off your horse," explained Chatfield. "We had to carry you in."

"And where is that assassin that was shooting at me?" demanded Morgan, suddenly remembering his approach to the ranch. "He's a Tolliver! I know it! They've followed me even here! But I'll kill him—I'll fight to the death!"

"No, no, Uncle," soothed Jim, "that was only Riley Sloper. He was out of his head with the heat."

"No, he wasn't!" denied Morgan. "I knew his father, well. The worst killer in the whole damned crew!"

"Well, he's gone," lied Chatfield, "so come in and wash up, Colonel. Don't you remember my father, Oliver Chatfield?"

"What? Oliver's son?" exclaimed the old man incredulously. "Why, of course I know you now! Why, Jim, I'm glad to see you. You must tell me about my old friend."

He shuffled along after him, talking garrulously about his father and quite diverted from his purpose; but as the door closed behind him Riley Sloper appeared and beckoned Horse-Ketchum outside.

"Ain't that Frying-pan George?" he asked mysteriously. "Well, this puts me in a hell of a fix. I done called off our feud—and I meant it, too. But if that old man finds out I'm one of Bodie's men, he'll go to shooting, instanter. And I'd shore hate to kill a Chatfield, now."

"Wait a minute," said Johnny. "Are you strong enough to ride?" And he slipped in for a word with Jim.

"He'll stake you to a horse," he reported. "But you'll have to leave your guns behind."

"I'll leave anything," promised Sloper, "not to break my word to Jim, after all this bad blood and killing. I'm a changed man now and I'm going back to Kaintuck to tell 'em about Little Jim."

"Come on, then," nodded Lightfoot, "and I'll give you an Indian pony." But as he was leading out the horse Morgan's quick ear heard its footsteps and he thrust his shaggy head out the door.

"You'd better be drifting," advised Horse-Ketchum quietly, holding the pony for Riley to mount; and Sloper swung up into the saddle.

"Who is that man?" demanded the old man sharply, squinting after him with purblind eyes. "Why, that isn't Riley Sloper!"

"Yes it is," answered Lightfoot. "He came back to get his horse. Good-by, Riley!" And he waved his hand.

"Hell and destruction!" raved Morgan, making a run to find his guns. "That's a spy! He's a Bodie man! Jim Chatfield, come out here and shoot that scoundrelly whelp!"

But Chatfield was nowhere to be found, and Sloper went whipping up the road.

"Lord A'mighty!" wailed the old man as he rushed out to the gate, "he got away, in spite of me! Why, that hound of a Tolliver has thrown in with Val Bodie in order to get his revenge. And now, by the gods, he'll ride back to Mormon Lake and tell Bodie the way is clear!"

"What way?" inquired Chatfield, coming out with his gun. And the old man screamed with rage.

"Why, the way to my mine!" he shrilled. "The way to the Lost Breyfogle, the richest mine in the world. Ride after him, Jim, and kill him!"

"I can't do it," responded Chatfield. "He's a Tolliver, Uncle, and I've promised never to fight them again."

"Then I'll ride him down, myself!" raved Morgan, running back to saddle his horse. But as he swung up to mount, the exertion overcame him and he fell back, senseless, on the ground.

"Poor old man," said Jim. "He's crazy."

But, for the first time, Horse-Ketchum doubted it.

CHAPTER XXVIII

THE HONEY-POT

TO Chatfield, to Damaris—even to Diana, his daughter—Randolph Morgan seemed out of his head. But Horse-Ketchum had seen the gold that he dug and he knew that his fears were sound. Riley Sloper had fled up the trail towards Mormon Lake, and if he even mentioned the presence of Frying-pan George, Val Bodie would guess the rest. For if Morgan had left his canyon, the gateway lay open—and the madman who guarded the heights was gone.

Lightfoot paced about uneasily as the women and Chatfield sought to pacify the stubborn old man, and at last he went into the room.

"I'll go back to your mine," he offered. "And hold it until you come."

"No! I'll go back myself!" stormed Morgan. "I'm perfectly well! Let me up!"

"No, Uncle!" protested Damaris, "you've had a hard fall and injured your head on a rock. And besides, you couldn't stand the heat. Now just lie down and be still."

Morgan lay back with a groan, but as evening came on he sent word for Horse-Ketchum to come.

"Young man," he began, "I am informed by my nephew that you are a person of some integrity.

Perhaps my daughter was to blame, in part, for your conduct—can I trust you to hold my mine?"

"You can if you treat me right and quit talking about your daughter!" answered Lightfoot, glancing at Damaris. "But if you folks say much more about my conduct, and Diana, I'm going to step up on my horse and *go!*"

"Oh, now, Mr. Lightfoot," spoke up Damaris reproachfully. "Just because I happened to warn her not to go too far—is that any reason to complain? You know that poor Diana has spent her life in that narrow canyon, without any mother to advise her; and I consider it my duty to take a mother's place and tell her about the ways of the world."

"Well, doggone it, can't you trust me?" he flared back, angrily. "We were getting along fine—we were friends. But now, every time I look at her she blushes and runs away. What have I ever done, more than kiss her once or twice, that time when her old man tried to kill me? I reckon I've got a right to *talk* to her, haven't I? Well, I haven't spoken a word to her, today."

"Diana is very tired," stated Damaris, "and Jim and I thought she should rest. But we didn't ask you in to discuss our cousin's affairs. Uncle Randolph wants to talk about his mine."

She waved her hand towards the old man, who was listening impatiently, and dragged Jim out of the room.

"Never mind her!" spoke up Morgan, "she's only a woman. Now what do you know of my mine?"

"It looked good to me, when I was up there," replied Lightfoot. "And Diana showed me some of the ore."

"She did!" exclaimed Morgan. "But never mind—never mind! Do you think that Val Bodie will steal it?"

"If he hears that canyon is open he'll be up it like a shot. That's why I say I'd better go and take care of it."

"Yes, but what assurance have I that you won't keep it for yourself, and put me to the trouble of evicting you? I remember you now, suh, and you came into this country on purpose to look for the Breyfogle!"

"Sure did," admitted Johnny. "But I didn't look any further after I'd seen a piece of your ore. I could have stole the mine then, if I wanted to."

"You could not!" glared Morgan. "And for the very good reason that I was there, and in full possession. Moreover, my claim is staked and I've kept up the assessment work. And if you'd tried to take possession I'd have killed you."

"You came damned near doing it, as it was," retorted Lightfoot. "Now what do you want me to do?"

"I want you," said Morgan, "to convince these folks that I'm not out of my head. And then we'll go back to the canyon."

"You lie down and go to sleep and quit arguing the matter and they won't need any convincing," replied Johnny. "And the way things are breaking I'll be glad to go along with you. In fact, I was about to go, anyhow."

"They're just crazed by the heat, and the excitement," confided Morgan. "Don't you mind what Jim's wife has to say. She's a good-hearted woman, but bossy, like all of them. Let 'em talk—it don't hurt—and then go ahead and have your own way."

"I'll remember that," promised Lightfoot grimly. "What time do you want to start?"

"At midnight," winked Morgan. "While they're all asleep. And young man, I'll tell you what I'll do. You stand by me faithfully in this racket with Val Bodie and I'll give you that horse you stole. Yes, Paynim—sired by Selim, out of Neysa—two of the finest English thoroughbreds in the Stud-Book."

"I'll go you on that," responded Johnny, shaking hands. But the old man would not let him go.

"One thing more," he said. "Leave that Injun at home. He's a Shooshonnie, and the whole breed is treacherous. In horses and men alike I've never known it to fail—a low strain is always base. It's blood that counts—and by the way, Mistuh Lightfoot, that's a good old Southern name you have. Would you mind telling me a little about your people? The pardonable anxiety of a father, you understand. I'm still concerned for the welfare of my daughter."

"Well, my old man was a lawyer in Austin, Texas, and he tried to make a lawyer out of me. That's all—except that I ran away."

"I see," observed Morgan. "And you're not a fugitive from justice?"

"I never look behind me!" answered Horse-Ketchum bluntly. And the old man clapped him on the shoulder.

"Enough said!" he nodded. "You're the very man I want. We'll start for the canyon at midnight."

Johnny slipped out the door and made his way to the corral, where the horses were kept up for the night; but though Paynim came forward and whickered eagerly, he put his rope on High Behind. He was a rough horse and an awkward one, with his high rump and straddling gait; but he was his own, and Johnny took him. He had decided to leave anyway, and another bout with Bodie would only serve to work off his spleen. But as he lay in the hay, awaiting the hour to start, he gazed at Paynim and sighed.

A thoroughbred, sired by Selim, with a pedigree that went back to Darley's Arab and likely the Godolphin Barb! And he had taken him for a mustang—a broom-tail! Once more he remembered the ecstasy that had thrilled him as he watched Paynim come galloping across the lake. How his mane had floated out as, like a creature of the night, he had led his *manada* to the water-hole! And with what a wild whistle he had greeted the mustangers when they whipped in to make their throws! But the horse never lived that could outrun Paynim. Yet Johnny had tied to him, at last.

What a fever he had lived in through these long months that had followed—of chasing and racing and skirmishes with Bodie, and flights for his life from Morgan! It was a rough country and a hard one, with no law but the knife and gun; but he had won, only to lose at the end. What Morgan's rifle and barricade had failed to accomplish, Diana's relatives had achieved in a day. She was afraid of him now, abashed in his presence—ashamed, perhaps, for what she had done. And so, by their talk, they had destroyed her childish innocence as ruthlessly as trampling on a flower.

But she was the same Diana still, this simple child of nature who had kissed him as if he had been her own brother; a creature of joyous moods and wild, lawless impulses, but kind and generous to a fault. What a pity that they had plucked her so ruthlessly away from him, with stern warnings against all mankind! And now he must go away and let her blush unseen until the memory of her innocence had lost its pang. But she would never be the old Diana again, with her childish longings to be loved.

Horse-Ketchum sighed and stretched out for a little sleep before the long, hard ride to Devil

Canyon; and then, as the Dipper rose high in the north he roused up and saddled the horses. Morgan came out bringing his rifle and six-shooters, which he had retrieved from Chatfield's room; and, leading out their mounts, they rode off up the trail that led to Enúpi Gai. He who twice before had fled from Morgan's vengeance now rode beside him, armed.

If Val Bodie arrived first there would be a battle or a killing—a plain murder at the mouth of the canyon. For Bodie could not prove a clear title to the mine while Randolph Morgan lived, and the shortest way for him was the one he would take— a cold-blooded assassination at the gateway. They rode fast, for the valley floor had cooled at last as the cold air from the upper country sucked down into the sink, forcing out the superheated vapors. The terrible heat had passed and as he saw his mountain before him the devil-man's obsession returned.

"They'll be there—I know it!" he cried again and again as they loped along through the night. "They've set out to rob me, the whole, devilish crew! But a Morgan never surrenders. If they've taken my mine, I'll take it back or know the reason. And if I get there first I'll blast down the north wall and block the gateway again."

"All right!" responded Horse-Ketchum. "Only let me get out first. All I ask is an open road—and Paynim."

"He's a noble horse," praised Morgan. "One horse in a million. A horse with the courage of a man. But I sized you up rightly the first time I saw you—you're a man that loves a horse!"

"That's right," agreed Lightfoot. "And I'll take good care of him. I wouldn't bring him on this trip, because the bullets will be flying. I've felt it in my bones, from the first."

"Then whip up that deformed creature and show some speed," cursed Morgan. "There's a fortune at stake, so ride! What a damned imposition, to keep me lying there in bed while that spy was riding back to Bodie! She's a Tolliver, that woman—I distrusted her, from the start! And she leads Jim Chatfield around by the nose as if he had lost his wits. Why, just a word from him and she'd have gone back where she belonged and left men's affairs to her betters. Whip up, I say, and ride!"

He put Turco to a gallop and Johnny followed close, while the old man cursed and raved. His giant strength had returned, and his fiery hatred of opposition, and Lightfoot kept discreetly in the rear. He was taking a chance, riding out with this madman who twice before had attempted his life; but chances were what men lived by in that Valley of Death and they rode until the dawn touched the east.

The knife-like edge of Devil Mountain stood out clear against the sky as they came within sight of the lake; but Lost Valley was empty and deserted.

Across the alkali flats to the west the wild burros came plodding in, and a raven flew down from the cliffs. He passed low, with rushing wings and beady black eyes, looking them over like the ghoul he was; but Morgan did not follow his flight. His desert-trained eyes were searching the wide valley and at last he pointed to the north.

"There go my horses," he exclaimed, "pulling out for Mesquite Spring. The feed's short up the canyon, and they've been shut up all summer. Let's ride up and turn them back!"

"What's the matter with going up the canyon first?" suggested Johnny. "You can round up your horses, any time."

"That's not as easy as you think," replied Morgan shortly. "This is the second time they've turned wild. They love the open country and may be gone for months. They're racers, and they're bound to have their run."

He took after them furiously, recking nothing of Turco's weariness as he spurred him across the water-soaked flats; but at sight of their master the golden horses hoisted their tails and sped away in full flight. Horse-Ketchum followed reluctantly, ready to aid in the drive if Morgan happened to turn them back; but they fled before his charge, kicking their heels up mischievously, and Turco lagged further behind. He raised his head and neighed as he saw his beloved companions setting forth on their gay adventure; but the hard gallop had sapped his strength and when Horse-Ketchum rode up he only grunted at the bite of the spurs.

"They've quit me!" yelled Morgan, whirling his horse to look back. And then, while he stared, his jaw fell.

"My God, what's that?" he cried, "coming down out of Daylight Canyon? It's Val Bodie—they're after my mine!"

He pointed a tremulous finger and Horse-Ketchum saw them riding, a long procession of horsemen, rushing down out of the eastern canyon and up across the washes to the north. They rode hard, dwarfed by distance till they looked like a column of ants on their way to some new-found honey-pot. And up in front, on his bay racer, Val Bodie led the gang as they swarmed into the mouth of Devil Canyon.

CHAPTER XXIX

"LAW!"

THROUGH his own bullheadedness, Morgan had thrown away his chance to become the defender of his mine. He had ridden off instead to turn back his runaway horses, and now he had lost them both. In a paroxysm of rage he sat watching the claim-jumpers as they poured into the mouth of the canyon, while his beard wagged in time to the gusty oaths that flowed from his mouth in a torrent. He cursed the horses, and Turco, and Jim Chatfield's woman who had kept him in bed like a child; and then, whipping Turco until he lashed him into a fury, he headed for Devil Canyon at a gallop.

Horse-Ketchum followed after him, debating in his mind whether to turn back or see the thing through. If they had gained the canyon first, Morgan's berserk rage would have served a useful purpose. With his rifle and six-shooters, and his name for a fighter, he could easily have turned back the Night Riders. But now he was charging into the mouth of a canyon that was defended by sixteen gunmen, the most desperate killers on the desert. Lightfoot lagged behind dubiously, scanning the cliffs for an ambush, but Morgan plunged boldly in.

In a long, expectant silence, Horse-Ketchum awaited the volley which would spell the old man's end. When it came he would know that Bodie had accomplished his purpose, but the only sound was the clank of shod hoofs. They had passed in, all of them, unawares of the devil-man's presence, intent only on the rich loot ahead; and after a long minute of waiting Horse-Ketchum leaned forward and jumped High Behind into a lope.

The way was clear, and Morgan still had a chance to gain back his treasure and his mine. But he could not win alone—the odds were too great—and Lightfoot had promised his help. For the horse that he loved he had given his word to ride with Randolph Morgan to his mine; and now, with all danger of ambush past, he spurred in to do his part.

Up the narrow, crooked passageway, with its towering walls on both sides, he followed on the jump. But as he approached the cave there was an outbreak of shooting and two riderless horses dashed past. Lightfoot gave them the trail, his pistol balanced to shoot, if the battle came his way. Then as the loud bang of a horse-pistol set his heart to pounding wildly he whooped and charged out into the open.

Before the mouth of the cave a group of men stood peering in. The ground was strewn with the plunder they had taken. But at sight of Horse-Ketchum, riding in from down the canyon, they broke and ran for the rocks. Then from inside the cavern the shooting broke out afresh and two men came rushing forth. Lightfoot whipped out his six-shooter and met their charge with a smashing bullet which threw up the dust at their feet, and they dropped their guns and ran.

There was a panic in the canyon, with men running to and fro and frightened horses splashing madly through the creek. And from within the dark cave a succession of muffled shots told Johnny that Morgan still lived. He came out on the instant, a smoking horse-pistol in each hand, stooping low to escape the expected shots. But at sight of Johnny, still mounted on High Behind, he straightened up and looked swiftly around.

"Oh! You here, eh?" he grunted, thrusting one pistol into its holster while he shoved cartridges into the other. "The rascals were looting my home. Look at these sacks of ore that they had lugged out into the open and thrown away to hunt for more gold. But there are two of them inside that will never steal again. Ketch my horse—we'll go up to the mine."

Lightfoot rounded up Turco, who had gone down to drink; but his brain was still in a whirl. Was it possible that one old man could whip single-handed this whole gang of thieves and claim-jumpers? He had scattered a good half of them at his first reckless charge. But where was Bodie— and Boots?

"Mr. Morgan," he warned, "you want to look out, now. Because Bodie is up at the mine."

"That's why I'm going up there!" returned Morgan tartly. "If you're afraid of getting killed— stay behind!"

"I'm not afraid," answered Johnny. "But Bodie will hear this shooting. And the Boots boys are up there, too."

"What do I care for them, the half-Injun whelps!" cursed Morgan as he swung up on his horse. "Val Bodie will fight—he's a white man!"

"Yes, and Hank Boots will fight!" put in Horse-

Ketchum. "Do you figure you can handle them both?"

"Well—you come along and tend to Hank," proposed Morgan, "and I'll tell you what I'll do. The whole gang will be up there, and they'll fight to hold that mine. But we can whip 'em if I can just down Bodie. Now you watch Hank—and I'll do the rest. If we win, you get half the mine."

Lightfoot stared at him curiously, for the crack-brained old prospector had suddenly been transformed into a strategist. The light of battle was in his eyes, he moved about quickly—and for the first time since Johnny had known him he seemed sane. Yet the odds were all against them, for every one of the Boots boys could shoot. They had been educated by their father for just such emergencies, and the chances were they would shoot on sight.

"What's to keep them from potting us with their rifles?" he demanded, "before we get close enough to shoot? I'm in favor of going up on foot."

"Young man," began Morgan, "I'm experienced in these matters, I'd killed men before you were born. Now you ain't hired to think. You do what I say and I'll give you half my mine."

"To hell with the mine," retorted Horse-Ketchum. "What good will it do me if I'm dead? I claim those Injuns will fight—"

"Let 'em fight!" stormed Morgan. "What the devil will we be doing? But I know Bodie, and he'll want to make a talk. And once I get him talking I'll walk closer. You stay on your horse, like you wasn't called in on it—you're a witness, while I stake my mine. But when you hear me say: 'Law!' you tend to Hank Boots. Because right then I'm going to kill Bodie."

He nodded his head and turned imperiously away and after a moment's hesitation Horse-Ketchum rode after him, for he could not go back on his word. Yet as he rode up the canyon he felt like a leaf, drawn in behind the rush of horses' feet. He had not counted on a battle so desperate when he had offered to go to the mine, nor would it have been necessary if Morgan's runaway horses had not diverted him from his purpose. Once safely inside the gateway, they could have withstood the charge of a hundred outlaws like Bodie, but the cards had fallen against them and now, willy-nilly, he was being drawn into a fight to the death. For Bodie and Hank Boots would shoot, and so would Boots' half-breed sons. But Morgan rode out against them blithely.

Up the canyon the cloudburst had swept away the trail that led to the hidden mine, but as they rounded the point and turned up the side canyon they saw Bodie at the tunnel's mouth. He stood waiting, his rifle ready to shoot; but Morgan came on confidently, ignoring Hank Boots and his sons. Always before, as Frying-pan George, he had been loudmouthed and violent, full of windy threats against the first man that jumped his mine. But in the presence of the actual jumpers he was calm. Bodie watched him narrowly—and Horse-Ketchum, riding behind—until they came to the edge of the claim. Then he stepped out and held up his hand.

"Stop right there!" he ordered. "You're trespassing on my ground." But Morgan rode in on him arrogantly.

"You're a dodrammed liar," he answered. "I've owned this mine for years."

"Hey! Stop!" yelled Bodie, whipping his gun up to his shoulder, "or I'll bore you through and through. There wasn't a stake or monument on the whole damned claim. And what's more, it's never been recorded."

"That's all right," argued Morgan, "I've got a witness here to prove that the claim was legally staked. That cloudburst came down and washed my monuments away. I order *you* off of *my* ground!"

He stepped down off his horse and advanced across the open; while Lightfoot, like a man in a dream, edged his horse out of the line of fire. It was impossible to believe that Morgan planned an open attack, that at any moment he might draw and fire. But Horse-Ketchum had seen him at the battle of the cave and he set himself for the fray. For before Morgan fired, if he lived up to his promise, he was to speak the one word: Law.

Bodie stood there, huge and glowering, his rifle ready to shoot, his henchmen lined up at his side.

Hank Boots, tall and lanky; Big John, with Pete behind him; and Injun Boots, black and evil-eyed. They were startled by the actions of Frying-pan George, and Hank Boots had cocked his rifle. But Morgan came on, oblivious of them all, his fierce eyes fixed on Bodie.

"Val Bodie!" he began, "you've been trying for ten years to rob me of my mine. But I tell you, right now, I won't stand it!"

Boots spoke in Bodie's ear, and his big rifle came up.

"Halt!" he commanded, "you murdering old renegade! You ain't got no mine! I done located it, I tell you!"

He stopped, and his gunmen spread out. A sudden hush came over them all, and Johnny knew the moment had come. They were set to shoot the old man down. Randolph Morgan sensed it, too; but he did not give an inch.

"You Mormon whelp!" he cursed. "You think you can steal it, do you? I came into this country before there was any law—" He leapt aside as he spoke the word and Horse-Ketchum saw Hank Boots lay his cheek against the stock of his rifle. Then Morgan's pistol went off and Johnny drew and shot before Boots could pull the trigger. Their two shots rang out like two cracks of a whip and Bodie and Hank Boots staggered back. Bodie swayed and fell sidewise, Boots toppled over backwards, and his three half-breed sons stood alone. Horse-Ketchum caught a glimpse of their evil, staring eyes as they ducked and went for their guns. Then High Behind rose up in a resistless, whirling buck and Johnny felt himself hurled to the ground.

He lit hard, dropping his pistol; but as he leapt up to a crouch he saw the Boots brothers, running. Morgan had charged them intolerantly, contemptuous of their rifles; and as Lightfoot looked up he saw Injun Boots fall, then turn over and whip out his gun. Big John and the youthful Pete were fleeing together down the hill, when with the vengeful swiftness of a rattlesnake Injun Boots aimed and fired, shooting Morgan in the back as he passed.

It was all over in an instant, and as Morgan fell Horse-Ketchum groped about for his gun. A bullet ripped down his shoulder-blade, burning its way like a streak of fire, and he rose up to find Injun Boots fanning. It was a trick he had learned from his renegade father, holding the trigger back firmly while he aimed from the hip and worked the hammer with the flat of his left hand. A second bullet struck Johnny, whirling him around and destroying his aim; but he came up shooting and, as they closed in to fight it out, Injun Boots stumbled forward and fell. But Johnny had seen the trick by which he had shot Morgan and he turned and emptied his gun. Then a giddiness seized him and he seemed falling through infinite space, until suddenly his light went out.

CHAPTER XXX

DIANA DECIDES

ALL the devils from hell seemed to be working on Horse-Ketchum, seering his back with a rod of fire, smashing his ribs in with mighty blows, choking his breath off until he struggled and woke up. He was lying alone before the mouth of Morgan's mine—the others who sprawled there were dead men. He gazed about dumbly, wiping the dirt from his bloodshot eyes, and from the distance a lost horse neighed. It was Turco, still waiting for his master.

A battle had been fought, but the vanquished had fled and the sole survivor lay weltering in blood. There was a trench plowed down his back, and at every labored breath a broken rib stabbed into his side, yet as he reared up he cursed the folly of it all. What to him was the Lost Breyfogle, when for one drink of water he would give his hope of salvation? It had not been his quarrel—he had been drawn into it against his will—and now Morgan and Bodie were both dead. Two more names added to the long list of men who had perished in the search for its gold. And Hank Boots and his son made four.

Like the dancing figures of a fever dream, Lightfoot envisioned once more the swift action of that desperate fight—Bodie and Hank Boots shot down together, outguessed at their own game, and then Morgan's overweening charge. But the cunning of Injun Boots had given him a quick revenge for the death of his father and Bodie. He alone had kept his head—and as Morgan fell he had turned his spitting pistol on Horse-Ketchum. There was nothing for Lightfoot then but to shoot. But now that it was over he felt sick.

The horse whinnied again and Lightfoot called to him hopefully. Then as Turco refused to come he crawled down towards him slowly, one hand pressed tight against his side. It was the broken rib that hurt him, but each time he stopped Turco whinnied a frenzied appeal. It was his nature to be loyal and, now that his master was dead, he had transferred his allegiance to Horse-Ketchum.

Turco was standing in the wash where at the first outbreak of shooting he had been stampeded by the frightened High Behind. But old High Behind had never stopped, for once before at Night Water he had felt the raking impact of buckshot, and Turco waited alone. It cost Lightfoot many a groaning to crawl up on his back and ride back to the deserted cave; and there, as Turco turned his head down the canyon, Johnny read what was in his heart.

Far below in the wide valley his brethren were running free, seeking out a new range to the north; and, loosening the saddle, Lightfoot stripped off the bridle and slapped him over the rump with the reins.

"Go ketch 'em, old boy," he said. "I wish I was going with you." And Turco set off, though doubtfully. He paused and looked back—then in a quick, joyous gallop he dashed away down the trail.

Horse-Ketchum stood alone in the deserted canyon, one hand against his side, a single gun on his hip; and in the distance he heard men's voices, shouting. Somewhere among the rocks or up on the lofty cliffs the scattered Night Riders were calling. He dodged into the cave, where amid the ruins of Morgan's home two dead men lay against the wall, and came out with a sack of jerked meat. Then, filling a canteen, he crept back into his old hiding-place and dragged out his tracks behind him.

In the battle at the mine he had come off victor, since he alone had survived; but if, sick and wounded, he fell into the enemies' hands, there would be a different story to tell. In the cool darkness of the cave, he stretched out behind the packboxes which had given him cover before; and after a drink from the canteen he fell into a fevered sleep, interrupted by the sound of passing footsteps. Harsh voices came to his ears and the clack of horses' hoofs. Then as night came on and the bats fluttered forth the ancient stillness returned.

He was awakened by the padding of velvety feet, the swift scurrying of some animal in his cave; and as he opened his eyes he saw a fox running out, while another stood gazing at him curiously. It was Christopher and Columbus, Diana's pet foxes—they had scented his jerked meat and come in. Or had they some remembrance of a former friendship, expressed by the faint wagging of their tails? Johnny tried to sit up, to reach behind him for the meat-sack, but his back seemed clamped in a bar of iron. The bullet furrow had become stiff, and the pain in his side made him wince and gasp for breath.

He lay back muttering, cursing the luck which had led him to this spot. Once before, filled with buckshot, he had awakened in this same cave and seen the bats flapping home with the dawn. But now there was no Diana to tend his stiffening wounds—he was alone, and his enemies were about. The foxes raced to the door as two horses came hammering up, and from his couch Horse-Ketchum could see their eager heads outstretched as they sniffed the wind from below. Then Christopher, the boldest, stepped out into the light, wagging his tail and whimpering softly.

"H'lo!" hailed a rough voice; and the foxes scurried away as swift as two flashes of light. One moment they had been there and the next they were gone. Lightfoot reached for his pistol and waited. Then silence, the sound of distant footsteps coming closer, and a head peered into the cave. It was Diana, and she was crying.

"Oh, Johnny!" she called. "Johnny, dear!" And Horse-Ketchum felt suddenly confounded. Diana had followed after him, but how could he meet her—how tell her of her father's death? But at the tenderness in her voice, the quavering word of endearment, his heart leapt within him for joy. She loved him, and she would care for his wounds.

"Johnny!" she cried hopefully; and when he answered from his hiding-place she stooped and ran into the cave. "Oh, *are* you here, Johnny?" she sobbed as she reached gropingly towards the form on the old, familiar couch. "Is it really you, Johnny? Aren't you killed?"

"Nope—I'm all right," responded Lightfoot. "Just got raked by a couple of bullets."

She found him in the darkness and as her hands touched his cheeks she leaned down suddenly and kissed him.

"I'm so glad!" she sighed. "So glad you're still alive! And I'll never be mean to you again. But—but where is Father, Johnny?"

She asked the question bravely but Johnny could see she knew the answer, and he told his story bluntly.

"We had a battle at the mine and he was killed," he said. "But he got Val Bodie first."

"Oh, and then *you*, Johnny!" she hurried on. "Were you there in the fighting? And did Bodie's men try to kill you?"

"Sure did," admitted Horse-Ketchum. "But

that's all over now. Who was that I heard talking, outside?"

"It was Captain Jack," she answered. "But when he looked into the cave and saw those two dead men lying there he was scared and ran away. We thought they were you, and Father."

"Couple of Bodie's men," he explained. "They were robbing the house. But you'd better not go back there, Diana."

"No, no," she promised. "I'll stay right here with you till Cousin Jim gets in. Jack and I rode ahead—we had Paynim and Moonbeam. But why did you do it, Johnny?"

"I don't know," responded Lightfoot. "Seemed like luck was against me—and I couldn't let him come up alone. We'd've been all right, at that, but he saw your horses pulling out. And when we got back—there was Bodie!"

"Poor Father!" she sighed. "But I knew he'd get killed—I told him so, hundreds of times. They were terrible men to deal with!"

"The worst in the country," he agreed. "There's your little fox at the door."

She turned, and as Christopher ran forward to greet her she gathered him into her arms like a child.

"Oh, I'm so glad!" she sobbed. "And here's Columbus, too! Before I saw them I thought you were dead. Then they ran out of the cave and I remembered how they loved you, Johnny."

She pushed them both away and leaned down close to Horse-Ketchum, and then she laid her cheek against his.

"And I love you, too," she whispered. "I don't care what they say!"

CHAPTER XXXI

THE HORSE-CATCHING

JIM CHATFIELD came riding in, to protect his cousin's property and attend to the wounded and dead—and then Damaris, to be a mother to Diana. An adobe house rose up, to take the place of the old cave, and Diana appeared demurely in long skirts. Captain Jack brought his woman and camped among the willows, but Horse-Ketchum lived on in his cave. There as the bats winged in and out and the foxes came to greet him and beg for more meat from his store, he lay dreaming till his back got well. But it was Jim who tended him now.

Diana was changed, and every day as Lightfoot passed he could hear Damaris, talking to her. She was a good woman—a good mother to such as little Jim—but Johnny thought she talked too much. She had reminded him more than once that Diana was related to some of the best families in Kentucky, and Jim had shown him one diamond from the casket which Diana had snatched when she fled. It was large, and a pure, bluish-white. Yet Horse-Ketchum knew he was welcome, for Diana had a smile in her eyes. And of course he had saved the mine.

The Lost Breyfogle lay just as it was, after the cloudburst and the battle had swept over it. To Diana its black depths were haunted by memories of her father and his wasted life—and four men had died at its mouth. In other matters she deferred meekly to the judgment of her cousins, but she ordered the tunnel closed. And of course, after all, it was her mine—although Jim thought it ought to be worked.

There was talk already of a trip back to Kentucky, to celebrate the end of the feud, and Diana would need the money. For while she was there, of course, she would have social opportunities which had been denied her in Devil Canyon. Damaris gave herself up to an orgy of sewing and fitting, for Diana must look her best; and sometimes, in the evening, Lightfoot glimpsed the filmy gowns which now replaced her buckskin suit. But Damaris was always present and Johnny did not linger, though they always invited him to stay.

He was rebuilding the pasture fence, which the flood had swept away, and putting in a new gate and stile. It was just like the stile which had been there before, when Diana had given him the kiss. He often sat there in the evening while Paynim and Moonbeam came down to stand at the bars, and when they looked down the canyon and snuffed the wind he knew where their thoughts had strayed. Somewhere outside the portals which shut them in, their runaway companions were playing. They were racing across the playas of distant dry lakes or mingling with the mustangs on the plains, but some day they would all come back.

The cool of autumn came and as the heat-fever left his brain Horse-Ketchum felt a strange content. Why should he seek to placate the designing Damaris, or show resentment when she kept Diana close? Diana had kissed him and told him that she loved him, no matter what they said. She had placed her cheek against his, alone there in the cave, and told him he was very dear. And the look in her eyes was the same, only now it was hidden and veiled.

But now the open ranges were calling and he got out his plaited throw-rope. Diana did not need him in the canyon now, for Chatfield would protect her mine; but somewhere, running wild, were the nine golden horses, which she watched for day by day. Every evening, with her foxes, when the sun was swinging low Diana went up the trail to her old lookout on the cliff, but Johnny did not dare to follow. The motherly eyes of Damaris were never long off the foot of that trail, and she had her opinion of horse-hunters.

Johnny overhauled his saddle and put in new latigos and limbered up his *reata* with tallow. Then he whipped it on the ground to straighten out the kinks and made delicate casts at High Behind. And he, though he had twice proved a recreant before gunfire, stood his ground and snorted to go. He was a good horse and a tough one on the trail after mustangs, and he knew the signs of a hunt. But Horse-Ketchum did not go.

The moon was at its full, the favorite hunting time for mustangers, and a cool wind sucked up from below; but that evening as he came back from the pasture he saw Diana, skipping lightly down her trail. Her cumbersome skirts were held high—she came down gayly, almost dancing— and when she spied him she waved her hand. Johnny glanced at the house, where Damaris was getting supper, and hurried to meet her, for he guessed the news.

"They've come back!" she said. "I saw them— down at Night Water. I'll meet you at midnight, Johnny."

She slipped into the house and Horse-Ketchum walked on air as he sought the shelter of his cave. It was the old Diana, the Diana who had kissed him and dared him to ride through the night—and her eyes had been alight, like stars. All the chatter of Damaris had not altered her a whit, when it came to a ride on the lake. She had let her cousin talk; and now, like her father, she would go ahead and have her own way.

The foxes followed after him as Lightfoot went

down the trail with his saddle and rigging on his arm, and as he sat by the gate the horses came down and nudged him with pleadings to go. Then the moon soared up and shone down into the canyon and Horse-Ketchum's heart stood still. On such a night as this how could she deny him? And yet he could not ask for a kiss. They were hers, to give if she would.

She came at last, gliding silently in her moccasins and with her golden hair thrown to the wind. It seemed in a way the symbol of her freedom, like her buckskin leggings and short skirt.

"Oh, Johnny!" she sighed ecstatically, "I just couldn't stay at home! There were Turco and Selim and all of them! Just think of all the mustangers that have been trying to catch them—and every one came back!"

"I'll ketch 'em," promised Lightfoot, "if you'll let me ride on Paynim!"

"Why, of course! He's yours!" she answered joyously. "Didn't I give him to you, long ago?"

"Well, yes," he admitted. "But Jim and your cousin Damaris—"

"Oh, come on!" she cried. "Let's go!"

She scrambled lightly over the bars and put her bridle on Moonbeam, while Lightfoot led out Paynim; and then, closing the gate against the sulky High Behind, they rode away down the dark, moonstruck canyon. Across patches of moonlight they spied Christopher and Columbus, gliding ahead like silvery-grey shadows, and Diana laughed for joy.

"Isn't it wonderful!" she said. "Oh, I never was so happy! I was afraid they'd never come back!"

"I was going out after them," answered Lightfoot soberly. "Kind of shut-in-like—up in that canyon."

"We're out of it!" she exulted, jumping Moonbeam into a gallop and tearing away down the wash; and as Johnny leaned forward Paynim dashed up beside her and led on till they came to the dry lake.

It lay like a silvery sea, bathed in tropical moonlight, with the mystery of the desert brooding over it—smooth and hard as a race-track. And from far across the flats there came the braying of wild burros as they carried on their endless battles. Diana reined in panting, knee to knee with Horse-Ketchum as he peered out into the night, but he did not take her hand. Paynim had thrown up his head, eagerly snuffing the breeze, and from the distance there came a high, shrill whistle.

"Plumb wild!" he said. "They'll run like a black-tail—been chased all over Nevada. You'll never ride up to them, Diana!"

"Yes, I will!" she insisted. "I raised them from colts, Johnny. Just let me do it my way."

"Well—sure!" he agreed. "But they've turned wild, I tell you. You should have seen 'em when they ran away from your father."

"Oh, but Johnny!" she protested. "You know

they were frightened then. Take your hand off of Paynim's nose."

Horse-Ketchum obeyed reluctantly and across the empty lake-bed Paynim sent his high, challenging neigh. Another stallion made answer and in the stillness of the night they heard his loud, explosive snort.

"That's Turco!" spoke up Diana. "He's angry."

"Yes, and Paynim is angry, too," answered Lightfoot. "If they once start to fighting, I'm ditched, so you'd better ride in alone."

"No! Now, Johnny!" she pleaded. "I want you to be with me when we catch them and drive them home. I had it all planned out."

"Well, you'll have to plan again, then," returned Horse-Ketchum. "Because a wild horse don't like a man. We've got the wind on 'em now, but the minute they smell me they'll leave here like a bat out of hell."

"All right, then," she came back, "you tell *me* how to do it. I've known those horses all my life!"

"But I haven't," countered Horse-Ketchum, "and they haven't known me. And don't you ever think they'll let me ride up on them, because it's only six months ago that I trapped them by the water-hole and put my rope on Paynim. Now you ride out and get acquainted first, and give 'em a good run on the lake. And then I'll show up on the windward side and you lead 'em back up the canyon."

"All right, Johnny," she assented at last, "I suppose you must be right. Only—" She paused and looked wistfully into his eyes. "I wanted *you* to be with me," she ended.

"Yes, I know," nodded Horse-Ketchum. "We'll ride home together." And he reined his horse away.

Diana rode out slowly, her foxes coursing ahead, mad with joy to be out on the lake; and as the band of outlaws trotted out on the playa she broke into a joyous gallop. But like one horse they turned and fled and were swallowed up in the night, while she followed, calling their names. From the distance Johnny could see them as they stampeded off, their tails held high like flags and Diana hot on their trail. Then as Paynim fought his head Horse-Ketchum rode him across the lake and took shelter among the mesquites.

The runaways had turned wild—they were mustangs again—but Paynim and Moonbeam were the top horses of the bunch and they would not let them escape. There was a long, anxious wait as Diana rode after them and then, across the lake-bed the patter of running feet as they circled back from the north. With a rush, half in play, they wheeled and gamboled across the playa—a new mare, Cressida, in Moonbeam's place in the lead, Turco herding them proudly from the rear. At sight of his rival, Paynim's wide nostrils flared and he fought against the hackamore on his nose; but Lightfoot choked him down, holding him resolutely back, and his lost *manada* swept on.

Diana could turn them now, and as they headed towards the north, Johnny could see her, riding low. Only her golden hair, mingled with Moonbeam's flowing mane, revealed her presence as they came thundering past, and Lightfoot's heart leapt at the memory of that night when first he had seen her. The same moon was shining, the same splendor illumined the playa—but now Diana was his. She would never go back to Kentucky, with scheming, match-making Damaris.

He could hear her calling now as she slowed the horses down, edging closer and barring the way to the north; and as they circled and maneuvered, led on by the jealous Cressida, Moonbeam whinnied to her perfidious children. They had left her for this usurper, the consort of Turco, who had ever lived in fear of Paynim's teeth. But not forever could the deposed leader be restrained and as Paynim's *manada* passed again he scorned the biting hackamore and charged.

The time had come to make their drive, if drive them they ever could, and Horse-Ketchum gave his mount his head. But he too swung low, clinging to his neck like a bat, and Paynim rushed Turco, bawling. The *manada* was running and they kept on, faster and faster, as that well-remembered challenge rang out. And Turco, though he turned, did not dare to give battle when Paynim rose up to strike. With mouth open and teeth gleaming, his pounding hoofs smashing out, he drove his presumptuous rival in wild flight. Then, circling his little band, Paynim rushed them towards the canyon, and once more Moonbeam dashed into the lead.

Up the wide, gravelly wash and into the black-mouthed portals they went at a breakneck gallop, and as they entered the narrow canyon the over-hanging walls gave back the echoes of their thunderous flight. Horse-Ketchum rose up yelling as they swept past the house and found themselves stopped by the gate. He reined Paynim right and left, popping his rope-end like a pistol-shot as they made futile breaks to escape; while Diana, leaping off, threw down bar after bar until the way into the pasture was clear. Then they poured in, leaping the barrier; and as Moonbeam passed, Diana swung up on her back.

Horse-Ketchum rode in laughing and put up the bars. Diana circled and came flying back. Then she leapt to the ground and stood beside him, panting, while her arms crept up around his neck.

"Oh, Johnny!" she sighed, "I just can't live without you." And she drew his head down for a kiss.

Center Point Publishing
600 Brooks Road ● PO Box 1
Thorndike ME 04986-0001 USA

(207) 568-3717

US & Canada:
1 800 929-9108
www.centerpointlargeprint.com